I0779478

ANTLERS

By S. Everest

This book is only for those 18 years and older.

If you are a survivor of sexual assault, rape, torture, or kidnapping, *please proceed with extreme caution.* **This book does not have a true romance storyline.**

This book contains triggers that may be uncomfortable for readers, such as sensory overload, suffocation, heavy blood and gore, electroshock therapy, and a depiction of suicide by hanging.

Other triggers may be considered spoilers and will not be listed here. For a *full list* of triggers, please go to my website: severestbooks.com/triggers

PLAYLIST

Part One

Rattle – Bingo Players

Doomsday – NERO

Murder In My Mind – Kordhell

DLMD – Darren Styles, TNT, Technoboy, Tuneboy

Part Two

Paradox – Andromida

FØØL - INHUMAN Remix – GHØSTKID, Code: Pandorum

vendetta! – MUPP, Sadfriendd

HAPPY HUNTING – Wage War

Purgatory – ATLiens, SVDDEN DEATH

Part Three

742617000027 – Slipknot

Alpha & Omega – SWARM

Blue In The Face – Rezz, Shadient, fknsyd

Take Me to Hell – SWARM

PART ONE

My eyes in the cool air, watching as you float along the path.
Your brown hair swaying with each step, your stride effortless in
your guide. The curve of your back, the slow reach of each step.
I need you. I need to breathe you in.
I need to push myself past my limits to have you.
To keep you.
Your lungs were meant to breathe my air. Your mouth was meant
to taste my tongue.
Your skin was meant to lay against mine.
Both of us as one.
Heartbeat racing, pulse pumping, heat spreading, cock hardening.
My vice is you.
My transgression is you.
I will keep you in my sights. I will take you as mine.
You didn't quiet my demons. You made them come alive.

10:53 PM

Black-painted stalls lined the wall, the metal cool to the touch as my shoulder rested against the frame. Crossing my feet at the ankle, I leaned in, closing my eyes and sighing.

"Mir, are you okay?" My voice hovered slightly above a whisper, but the bathroom took my words and turned them into an echo. With one hand in my sweatshirt pocket and the other holding my phone, it felt like I waited an hour for a response.

"Yeah, I'm fine." Her words were squeezed out through a suppressed groan, and it was evident that it was a bold-faced lie. As I turned my back to the stall door, my head tipped against the metal, and I pursed my lips. I looked around the bathroom, studying its interior walls. Thankfully, it was well-kept and clean, unlike most public bathrooms I've been in. There was no slick grime on the floor, no trash hiding in the corners, and the sinks and their faucets seemed to be sparkly and shiny. And surprisingly, it smelled good. *What was that, citrus? Apple?* Whatever it was, it was doing a good job of masking the horrid smell of a restroom.

The walls, stalls, and doors were painted black, as was the floor, which had an intricate, white mosaic pattern. Fake, dim sconces were between the mirrors, illuminating the handwashing sinks and setting the dark mood before heading back outside.

I'd never been in a gothic bathroom before, but there really was a first time for everything.

I looked down at my black combat boots, kicking them against the floor before speaking again.

"You don't sound fine, Miranda."

Another groan sounded on the other side of the door, almost making me queasy, too. I frowned at the feeling.

A flush sounded from a few stalls down before someone opened their door and stepped out. It was a girl around my age, with dark—almost black—straight hair that was cut right to her shoulders. She sent me a quick, sympathetic smile as she pushed up the sleeves of her light grey fleece jacket and turned to the sink, beginning to wash her hands.

"You should go without me," Miranda said, and I straightened.

"What?" I asked, shocked. "But we drove all this way and already bought our tickets. And you know they don't give refunds."

"Exactly," she replied. "You should go. Get your money's worth."

I hesitated. "But…"

I bit my bottom lip as the girl at the sink finished washing her hands. Her dark brown eyes flicked to me in the mirror as she turned off the water. The thought of my night ending before even starting sobered me. I hated the idea of not getting to experience the most talked about attraction in the entire country.

"I can't," I began, my voice defeated. "There's no way I can walk through these houses without you. And I'm *definitely* not going alone."

After the girl at the sink grabbed a paper towel, she turned to me, her back against the white porcelain. I watched as she warred with herself, debate funneling through her like the water in the drain.

Then she spoke six words that would change my whole night.

"You can tag along with us," she finally said quietly. Her indecision quickly faded as she creased her hands in the paper, soaking up the excess water. "If you want."

Instantly, I shook my head. "Oh, thank you, but I can't leave her here alone." I hitched my thumb over my shoulder, referring to the sickness in the stall behind me.

After a brief, awkward silence, with me glancing at my phone and the girl throwing away her paper towel, Miranda spoke up through the door. "No, you should go. I'll meet up with you later."

Cinching my eyebrows, I turned to the door. "Miranda, I'm not leaving you."

The girl at the sink crossed her arms, politely waiting for my final answer. What kind of friend would I be if I just left her here in this— clean and oddly comforting—public restroom?

"Go. Please. One of us deserves to have fun." Miranda's words were cut short by another moan, and I could picture her bent at the waist, ready to hurl.

Looking over to the other girl, I took a deep breath. I knew this would be my only other opportunity to go, and with tickets over one hundred bucks a pop, the night did *not* come cheap. With a sigh of defeat, I dropped my shoulders and looked to the girl at the sink.

"Would it be okay? Just until she feels better?"

The girl nodded with a friendly smile stretched across her face.

With one final twist to the bathroom stall, I spoke loudly. "Text me as soon as you step foot out of this bathroom, okay? We can find a place to meet up."

The sink girl chimed in, leaning forward, the ends of her dark hair falling over the tops of her shoulders. "I don't think there's any cell service out here. At least, there hasn't been since we got here. You probably won't be able to call or text."

"Of course not," I replied over a wince, the realization hitting me hard. A pause settled as I kept my face turned to the stall, a thought appearing in my mind. "How about you go to the ticket booth when you're done in here? Maybe they can page or radio someone, and I'll come and get you."

But as the words left my mouth, the syllables trailing off and lingering in the air, I realized how dumb it sounded. We were in an abandoned park well after sundown, with hundreds of people in attendance. It was dark, it was crowded, and the place was so expansive that by the time I could meet her somewhere, it would be time to leave. Plus, the park stopped letting people in at eleven, which was only a few minutes away. And by the sounds of it, Miranda wasn't going to be out of here anytime soon. I shook my head again at the conclusion.

"Never mind. I'm sorry," I said, looking at the sink girl. "It was really nice of you to offer, but I think I should stay with her."

"Oh, stop," the voice sounded through the stall. "Would you go already? Just let me puke in peace, *please*." Miranda coughed, and I could hear her voice growing irritated. I didn't want to fight her anymore, and I really *did* want to go through these houses.

Sink Girl gave me a second glance as she turned to leave. Another older woman stepped into the building and made her way into one of the stalls, shooting us both a confused look.

"Wait, *wait*," I called to Sink Girl, who paused in the doorway and turned to me. I pushed off the stall and began to follow her, accepting her invitation. But before leaving, I turned back to the stall one last time.

"Okay, fine. I'll go. But I don't care if there's no cell service. You better at least *try* to text me when you're done in here. Got it?"

"Got it," Miranda said as Sink Girl and I stepped out of the bathroom in unison, side by side.

The autumn air was crisp and sharp as we walked down the paved path together. Lights illuminated the walkway as orange and brown leaves crunched under our feet with each step, the noise soothing to my ears. Sink Girl slid her hands into her light-colored fleece jacket and leaned her shoulder close to mine. "I'm Mia." Her voice was soft and airy, matching her friendly composure. Along with her jacket, she wore plain black leggings and brown knee-high boots. She was on the taller side, but she didn't completely tower over me.

I grinned. "I'm Sadie."

"Nice to meet you, Sadie." Mia showed a genuine smile before taking a deep breath. "So, your friend back there, is she okay?"

I shrugged. "She thinks it's something she ate. We stopped at a gas station on the way here to get some food, and I don't think it agreed with her."

Mia scrunched her nose, her expression showing a hint of compassion. "Yeah, gas station food is always a gamble. But when it's good, it's *so* good."

"Oh, absolutely." We both shared a friendly laugh together before reaching the crowd. There were people lined up at the ticket booth outside the gates before they closed at eleven. By the looks of the line, there was no way everyone would make it in time.

"Mia!" Someone shouted to our left at the park entrance, and Mia turned and smiled.

"This way." She motioned for me to follow, and I did. Weaving through the clusters of people, we came up to two guys who were patiently waiting, their bodies turned in our direction. They looked to be right around my age, with both of them glancing at me in confusion. One quickly wrapped his arm around Mia's shoulders, his dark hair matching hers, a lovesick shimmer in his eyes as he looked her way. Mia leaned into him, sharing that same look before turning back to me.

"Guys, this is Sadie. She's going to be hanging out with us for a bit."

"Oh, thank God I'm not the third wheel anymore," the other guy said, more to himself than to anyone else. I pushed a smile as he slid his hands into his jacket pockets.

Mia rolled her eyes, ignored his statement, and then turned to the guy clinging to her. "Sadie, this is Elliot," she said, patting his chest as he lifted a hand in a wave. Then, she motioned to the guy standing next to me. "And this is Connor."

Connor dipped his chin and nodded slowly, and I didn't miss the way he tilted his smile, letting the introduction linger a moment too long.

My eyes involuntarily locked with his, the bright blue irises searching me, a small crinkle in the outer corners forming from his easy expression. "Nice to meet you, Sadie," his voice rattled off as his eyes left mine to quickly scan me, his gaze trailing from my black boots to my black, ripped jeans and up to my thin, dark grey sweatshirt. I gathered my long, wavy brown hair in one hand and pulled it all over my right shoulder, suddenly nervous that I had invaded this close-knit friend group on a night out. After snapping out of his short trance, Connor's eyes found mine again as he sucked in a breath. "Do you usually come to haunted houses alone?"

"Oh, no," a timid laugh found its way out of me. "My friend got sick. Mia was kind enough to invite me to tag along."

"That's my girl," Elliot squeezed Mia's shoulders, giving her a proud grin before softly kissing her on the lips. "Always looking out for people."

I didn't have to look to feel Connor's eye roll, and I almost joined him. Before I could say anything, Connor leaned toward me, his hand shielding his mouth in a hidden secret. "Don't worry, they're like this *all* the time. We'll be lucky if they only kiss once every *five* minutes instead of once every *two*." His posture insisted on secrecy, but his volume didn't hide anything. I laughed, sparking another golden smile out of him.

"Well, should we head in?" Elliot asked, ignoring Connor's jokes before looking to me. "You have a ticket, right?"

I pulled a thin, white rectangle out of my hoodie pocket and gave it a slight wave. "Sure do."

"Good," he replied. "These things were a *bitch* to get."

Mia grumbled. "Especially since they only let in two hundred people *a night*. Can you believe they have a waiting list? There are *that* many people that want to see what this is about."

"Including us," Connor agreed.

Mia nodded. "And all those people waiting in line, hoping for their chance, will be turned away in a few minutes. What a bummer."

Turning to the gates, I tuned out their conversation and inhaled, trying my best to ignore the deep, tingly jitters bouncing in the pit of my stomach. I love haunted houses—always have—and the rush I get before stepping through the gates is like no other. I don't like heights and I definitely don't like bugs, but there's something about being scared that makes my blood run hot, filling me with a shot of adrenaline that's like a drug. I love chasing the thrill, chasing the high, and chasing the madness. My soul feeds off of it; my existence lusts after it. Slipping into a dark building with people lurking in the shadows, consuming peoples' fear, gives me an unstoppable heat.

A heat that spreads right to the area between my thighs, wrapping me in a slick desire that I hardly ever escape.

But that was my little secret to keep.

I looked up to the top of the black iron gates, and a slow smile spread on my lips as I read the name.

Inferno's Edge.

It's currently the most famous group of haunted houses in the whole country, with its name in constant headlines and trending daily during the Halloween season. Located on a secluded plot of land, visitors wishing to endure the horror have to drive up numerous back roads. There are no lights or street signs, only old wooden posts with painted arrows to help lead the way. Empty fields and dark forests cradle the dirt roads, giving no sign of life for miles.

There were no small towns. No houses. No mailboxes. No villages. Nothing.

The fact that the attraction was so isolated was like a cherry on top. The place was terrifying in itself, but when you throw seclusion into the mix, it only added to the fear.

The only ones to hear you scream are the ones that make you.

In the surrounding area, *Inferno's Edge* beats any competition in the span of one hundred miles, if not a thousand, before they ever have a chance to make a name for themselves. Most places will open for a season, allowing others a chance at wholesome Halloween fun when they're not waiting in line at *Inferno's Edge*. And even those who do make their own haunted house never make enough money to open again the following year.

Everyone wants to experience *Inferno's Edge,* even if they don't make it all the way through.

Rumor has it that *Inferno's Edge* is home to an area called "Alkene Caves." If there were any actual caves here, I wasn't sure. There have been whispers of the caves being part of one of the houses, with some people even getting lost in them, their screams getting sucked into the void as they were never to be seen again. But those were all just stories meant to scare people.

And it worked.

Inferno's Edge has been a popular attraction for over ten years, with the hype only escalating each year. Headstrong haunted house enthusiasts come from all across America to see what the hype is about, and no one ever leaves disappointed. With high-end actors and performers hiding out between houses, eerie sounds floating around the paths, and special effects catching your eye at every turn, the experience is heightened even when you're not expecting it. Sometimes, you'll be followed; sometimes, you'll be chased; sometimes, you'll even be cornered with nowhere to go. But no matter what, everyone loves it.

It's what we're all here for, after all.

And judging by the churro I bought when I got here, their food trucks are good, too.

But all of that is standard stuff. There's nothing new, nothing innovative about any of that. At the front of the park, orange jack-o-lanterns lined and illuminated the pathways, cooing ghosts floated over our heads on timed intervals, and motion-activated skeletons jingled their bones as people walked by. Clowns teased you, serial killers chased you with their chainsaws, and zombies with blood dripping from their lips begged to munch on your brain. But once you got deeper into the park and began to experience what the houses had to offer, those things slowly dissipated, and things seemed to turn more sinister.

So, what made this place so different? Why did everyone want to experience *this* version of absolute horror?

The answer comes from *inside* the houses.

There are five separate houses to walk through, all spread throughout the abandoned land: *The Asylum, The Vision, The Eternity, The Clouds, and The Night.* The themes change every year, so no one ever shows up knowing what to expect.

Sure, most things are a gimmick, considering it's Halloween season, and everyone wants to be spooked. But every single person who enters and exits these houses never leaves without goosebumps. There's something more than the cheap thrills advertised, and it's a known fact from haunted house-goers that it *isn't* all fake.

And that's what draws everyone here.

Not only do people want to be scared, but they want to be *terrified.*

They want to leave here in a cold sweat, their fears gnawing away at their insides, begging for escape.

With only two hundred people allowed in each night, most don't make it through all five houses. Seventy-five percent of guests make it to house two, forty percent make it to house three, fifteen percent make it to house four, and only five percent of guests enter the final house. And even then, some of those in the final house don't make it all the way through. They take a few steps in, then turn around and haul ass right back out.

Most of the time, the fear in the guests comes from something unexplainable. The reviews written about *Inferno's Edge* are all unable to describe the level of gut-wrenching horror they experience, stating that the mindset is completely unattainable unless it's lived through.

Ghosts? Maybe.

Witchcraft? Possibly.

Demons? Who knows.

A good ol' trick of the eye? An optical illusion, disguising as something unspeakable? Probably.

At least, that's what I'm betting on.

The only definite thing anyone ever takes away from *Inferno's Edge* is the desire to *never* come back.

And that makes the run of my blood pump even faster.

11:21 PM

Outside of the first house, *The Asylum,* was an outstretched line leading us to the beginning of our adventures. I could already hear the screams of scared girls flooding the outdoors, even though we were still somewhat far from the entrance.

"So, Sadie, are you from around here?" Connor asked as we stood in an awkward square, facing one another.

I lifted a shoulder in a half-shrug as I eyed him, his brown hair lifting with a slight curl, his blue eyes glinting in the moonlight. We took a step closer to the entrance. "Kind of. About an hour south of here, but it's an easy drive."

"South?" Elliot asked. "Whereabouts?"

"Petersburg."

"No shit," he replied, the others showing a face of recognition as well. "We live about twenty minutes south of you."

"Oh, really?" I asked with a smile, growing more comfortable with them as our time passed on. "Have you been here before?"

"Nope," Mia said with a pop of her lips as the other two shook their heads. "But we've been hearing about it for *years,* so we figured we'd give it a try."

"Do you know anyone that made it to the end?"

Mia replied, "I have friends who made it to the entrance to the second house but backed out before going in."

The line moved forward, and we all took a step closer to the building.

I glanced around to the three of them, eyeing them suspiciously. "I take it you guys don't really like haunted houses?"

Connor immediately shot a look to Elliot before laughing. "Some of us don't like to be scared."

Elliot rolled his head out of annoyance. "No, I would just rather stay at home with Mia. Scary movies are better than these cheap-ass haunted houses, anyway."

"Cheap?" I repeated, doubt heavy in my questioning, but Elliot paid me no mind.

We took another step closer.

Connor nudged him with his elbow. "How would you know? You haven't even stepped foot in one yet."

Leaning in, I interrupted before Elliot could answer. "Not to side with Connor here, but it *is* ranked number one out of the top ten haunted houses in America. It's *got* to be good to get that sort of status."

Connor glanced at me, the corner of his lips curling upward before he turned back to Elliot, raising his eyebrows. "See? You're in line for the top haunted house in America. Soak it in."

Right then, a guy with skin intricately painted grey, rotting teeth, and white contacts popped up over Elliot's shoulder, placing his face beside his. The group of us jumped, startled at the newcomer.

"Yeah, buddy, *soak it in,*" the creepy man hissed, his eyes wide and his smile sinister.

And then he disappeared, fading back into the darkness behind us.

With all of us looking at each other, a dreaded fear plastered on Elliot's face, we unanimously broke out in laughter. Elliot shook it off, trying but failing to laugh with us.

Connor and Mia poked fun at Elliot while my laugh quickly faded. With a slight slant of my brows, I felt a sudden layer of ice on my back, like a rush of cool air brushed against my skin. The sensation made its way up to the nape of my neck, like a breathless whisper in the dead of night. Goosebumps covered every inch of me, causing me to shudder, my body thrashing out a quick, hostile shake.

"Sadie," Connor looked at me. "You good?"

I nodded, and his stare lasted a beat before turning back to the others.

But the feeling was still there, like tiny pinpricks on my flesh, piercing and jabbing me with needle-sized icicles. Slowly and cautiously, I turned my head to look over my shoulder. My eyes scanned the short line behind me, not seeing anything out of the ordinary. Then, I glanced over my other shoulder. Out of the corner of my eye, a black shadow vanished beyond the crowd, out of sight, leaving only a dark haze in its wake. I blinked, trying to convince myself that what I saw was only a product of my imagination.

But the feeling on my back grew warm.

Heated.

Like white flames on my skin.

Whatever—whoever—was behind me sent volcanic waves down my body, leaving no room to wonder if I needed to be scared.

I knew I should *always* be scared.

Once I snapped back into the moment and continued through another ten minutes of small talk, we reached the front of the line. A group of teenage girls sauntered inside ahead of us, and they didn't make it three steps into the building before screaming, then laughing, then screaming again.

Hopefully, they can keep their happy spirits throughout the rest of the house.

In front of the entrance was a table with a stack of papers, a bucket of pens, multiple cardboard boxes, and two older women sitting behind it all. They weren't dressed up as actors and didn't seem to care much about the screaming behind them. They simply dressed warmly with smiles on their faces and flashing pumpkin pins on their sweatshirts.

"Hi all," one woman began. "This is a waiver for the remainder of the experience. Actors are allowed to touch you, but you are not allowed to touch them. No vandalization, no cameras, and no food, drink, or gum inside. We are not liable for any pain or injury that may occur. This applies to every house from here, forward. Any breaking of the rules will have you escorted out."

"I'm sorry," Elliot spoke up. "Did you say pain?"

The woman ignored him and pulled out four pieces of paper, handing one to each of us. Without reading it over, I assumed the paper stated the rules the woman just announced to us, but the length of the paragraph led me to believe I was signing up for more.

Much more.

After glancing at each other briefly, we all grabbed a pen and signed our names at the bottom, sealing our commitment to the experience. Once she collected our papers, she reached into the cardboard boxes, pulling out four sets of four bracelets. We each took a set and slipped them onto our wrists. Pinching them between the fingers of my other hand, I rubbed them, feeling the plastic jelly material sliding under my fingertips. They were color-coded: black, yellow, red, and green, and the words *"Inferno's Edge"* were printed in bold lettering on each of them.

"Since your ticket is your entrance to *The Asylum,* you only received four bracelets. After this, each house requires one of your bracelets for entry. Do not lose them, or else you will not be able to enter. No exceptions."

We nodded in understanding. Mia looked down at her own set of bracelets and pulled the green one between her fingers. "Look," she started, and we all looked down at her wrist. "My green one says *Edge's Inferno.*"

I peered down at my own bracelets, but they all had the correct wording. Elliot and Connor's must've been right as well because they didn't say anything. We all shrugged it off as the woman lifted her hand to the doorway, gesturing for us to proceed.

"Enjoy."

The single word sounded like it was etched with something wicked, but I cast it off to be just part of my nerves. With a thick amount of hesitation between us, we all looked at each other, unsure as to who should step inside first. Elliot shook his head, along with Mia, leaving Connor to look at me. He tilted his head playfully, accepting his fate with a knowing grin.

"Shall we show them how it's done?" he asked me through a whisper, his eyes captivating mine. I couldn't help the smile growing on my lips as I nodded my head. With his hand tucked in the pocket of his jacket, he extended his elbow to me, and I slipped my hand through, gripping the fabric.

The four of us stepped inside and were instantly swallowed into darkness. Mia grabbed onto my hoodie behind me, and I could hear the speed of both Mia and Elliot's breathing increase.

As we stepped in farther, the door slammed closed behind us, causing us all to jump. Elliot cursed under his breath as the small amount of lighting from the outdoors was taken from us, and the inability to see was jolting.

I could feel my heartbeat increase as the warm feeling began to consume me.

The need to be scared.

The need to fear for my life.

My survival mode was already kicking in, and this was only the beginning.

11:35 PM

THE ASYLUM

"You would think they would give some sort of warning," Elliot said to the group from the back of the line. I clutched onto Connor's sleeve tighter, my knuckles turning white in the darkness as complete silence surrounded us.

"Our eyes will adjust. Give it a minute," Mia said in a whisper, a heavy quiver in her voice.

With Connor growing tense under me, I could feel a shake of his head. "There's no way, it's completely—"

Before he could finish, I noticed something on the floor ahead of us, causing me to shake Connor out of his sentence.

"Look down," I spoke, and I could feel a small movement from him. There was a small red light on the floor, a pinhead dot, almost like a laser. Connor moved toward it, the rest of us instinctively following. Once we reached it, another red laser flickered on to the left of us. We turned to head in that direction, shuffling our feet in unison. Another red laser turned on to our right, and we all glanced over to it.

"Is this some sort of maze?" Elliot asked with a huff, clearly growing annoyed at the pursuit.

"I don't think so," Connor replied, still leading the line. Bumps and thumps sounded in the air as we knocked against the wooden walls, our feet stumbling as we tried to make our way through the darkness. We followed three more red lasers, taking us in multiple directions before Connor walked face-first into a wall, still unable to see anything in the dark.

"Dead end?" Mia asked.

I could hear Connor's hands sliding up and down the surface, looking for a way through. Once he was halfway down, I heard a jingle of metal, the sound filtering through my ears.

"It's a doorknob."

"Open it," I said quickly.

Right as Connor turned the handle, Elliot jumped, shoving Mia into my back and pushing me harder into Connor, which forced him to fall through the newly opened door.

"*Fuck*! Something touched me!" Elliot said, trying to get away from whatever it was as he rubbed the back of his neck. We all collectively laughed, except for Elliot, whose face was as white as a sheet.

But then I realized I could see his face.

I could see.

Letting go of Connor, I glanced around the wide, open room. It resembled an abandoned warehouse, with a few sporadic lights illuminating circles on the grey, concrete floor. It was completely empty, except for one thing.

In the middle of the room, under a bright ring of light, was a dark, wooden chair. In that chair was someone, a man, facing away from us. His hands were tied behind his back, and his head hung down low, his chin dipping close to his chest. He was dressed in an all-white straitjacket, white pants, and plain, white shoes to match.

I studied the room as dust kicked up at our feet, drying out the inside of my lungs. I coughed lightly into my free hand.

So, there was a guy sitting in a chair. What was supposed to be so scary about that?

With Mia huddling in close to me, she whispered, "Where do we go now?"

Ignoring her, I kept my eyes on him. My eyes stayed on his body through the open back of the chair, analyzing his ribs. I watched as his torso expanded, inhaling with a deep, slow breath.

"Over there," Connor said, jutting his chin to the other side of the room, where a small red laser dotted the floor. In order to get there, we had to pass the suspicious, quiet guy in the chair.

With all our eyes glued to him, waiting for the unexpected, we cautiously made our way alongside the wall, keeping our path slow and orderly. His dark, shaggy hair covered the side of his face, never allowing us to see him or him to see us. The others may have missed it, but I noticed his neck twitch ever so slightly, his head jerking to the side by only a fraction of an inch. He knew we were there without even looking at us.

His ribs expanded, then released.

Expand, release.

He was steady and even. His eerie calmness seemed to contradict whatever put him in that straitjacket.

We were halfway to the laser before the guy stood to his feet at an unnatural speed. With his knees locked and his hands still tied behind his back, the chair he was sitting on flung to the wall we were pressed against, shattering and splintering into dozens of pieces. All of us ducked down, our hands covering our heads in shelter.

"What the *fuck*?" Elliot yelled.

Pieces of wood rained down on us, sharp chips falling against our heads and shoulders.

"Go!" Mia shouted, and without a second thought, we all ran to the laser.

As we quickly made it to the other side of the room, with the laser pointing at our feet, I turned to take one last look at the space behind us. The chair was destroyed, and the guy remained standing in the middle, his shadowed face still cast down. I glanced at the wall, trying to see if there were any marks, dents, or scratches, but there was nothing. No chipped paint, no holes, *nothing*. The only thing on that wall was a mounted, eight-point deer head, looking straight ahead, hidden in the soft darkness.

I swallowed the rush of blood that was creeping up my throat.

The deer was out of place. It wasn't something that fit the haunted house narrative. It was obscure and hidden, like you could only find it if you were actively searching for it.

My pulse kicked up a notch, and I blinked all pause away as I brought my attention back to the group.

Connor easily found another door and didn't hesitate to bust through it. I grabbed onto the sleeve of his jacket and followed, feeling the steps of Mia and Elliot behind me.

"Holy shit," Connor said, slightly breathy. "That was…"

"In-*fucking*-sane?" Elliot finished.

"Terrifying?" Mia added.

Fantastic. The word ran through my mind as I took a deep breath, inhaling my adrenaline. The chair came only inches from our heads, and if we hadn't ducked, we would've been hit. The thought of being put in that position created a sudden wetness between my legs. I squeezed my thighs together, thankful we were back in the dark where no one could see me or the aroused look on my face.

At least, I *thought* no one could see me.

But the sudden raised hair on the back of my neck said differently. Someone was here, hidden in these black walls, with their eyes on me. It was the same feeling I had when we were outside, waiting in line.

I could picture *lips close to my ear.*

Breath over my shoulder.

Hands reaching for me.

Steps following mine.

I could picture it, but I couldn't *see* any of it.

Obviously, I knew Connor, Mia, and Elliot were here with me, but this presence felt different. It felt intense. It felt sharp and strong, even in the dark, and I knew that one piercing glance in the light would split me in half.

Part of me was thankful I couldn't see whose eyes were on me. I could act like I was oblivious to the whole thing, and no one would ever know.

We found ourselves in another room with another red laser at the bottom of the floor. This time, it led us to the left, taking us down a hallway that felt like it was never-ending. We walked, and walked, and walked in silence before reaching another laser, this time taking us to the right. It was only a few steps before we hit a wall, and Connor's hand instinctively moved to grab a doorknob.

Pushing it open, we were met with a blinding light, and all of us shielded and squinted our eyes in adjustment. Bright white tile spread across the floor and scaled up the walls. There was a white porcelain sink, cracked on the edge, along with a white toilet that had streaks of red liquid dripping down the sides. On the other side of the room was a white, clawfoot bathtub filled to the brim with a deep, crimson liquid. Red handprints and footprints were scattered throughout this bathroom; some marks even trailed up to the ceiling. The light of the intense LED bulbs shined off the gloss of the ceramic tile and burned into our vision, the contrast from the dark hallway making my pupils dilate in an ache. The door clicked closed behind us.

I felt like we had entered into a *Saw* movie.

Connor stepped in first, looking down at the bare footprints on the floor. I watched as he slightly cocked his head and furrowed his eyebrows, as if he was deep in thought. He then squatted down, studying the red footprint with his gaze before reaching and swiping it with his finger. The red liquid smudged, leaving a streak in its wake.

"It's fresh," he noted, looking at his finger.

"Thanks, *CSI*," Elliot replied. "How do we get out of here?"

The four of us glanced around the room, looking for some sort of exit. As my eyes fell to the sink, I noticed a small plastic deer figurine next to the faucet handles.

A deer with large antlers, just like the one mounted on the wall in the other room.

The sight of it sent a small tingle through my body, like it was a secret only I was supposed to know.

My fingers curled as I fought every urge to reach out and pick it up.

Who knows, maybe I was meant to. Maybe it was a clue to a way out of here.

But before I could read into it anymore, and before any of us could find any sort of exit, the red liquid in the tub began to shift. Our eyes met the rocking motion, our bodies still as we watched the sloshing of the liquid, some of it spilling over the sides. Slowly, a head broke through the surface, facing away from us. Connor stood back up as we stayed there, unsure of what to do or where to go.

All we could do was watch.

Hands reached up and gripped the edge of the tub, the fingers abnormally long and thin as they twisted around the side. The person used the tub as leverage to pull the rest of their body out from the bottom.

It was a young woman with long, dark hair slicked to the scalp, covered from head to toe in the blood that she was just submerged in. With her back still to us, she stood to her feet, her blood-soaked nightgown clinging to her slim body.

Connor reached his arm out and pushed me behind him.

Blood dripped everywhere, from the sides of the tub, from the hem of her gown, from the tips of her long fingers. Turning her head slowly, she lifted her leg and stepped out of the tub, creating a brand new footprint on the white tile.

"Fuck! *Fuck!* Where do we go?" Elliot shouted in a panic as he turned to open the door we came through, but it was locked. Connor moved and ran his hands along the white walls in desperation, looking for a way out. Mia followed suit as I remained frozen in the middle of the room. The woman turned the rest of her body, her gaze locked on me as she slowly brought her other leg out of the tub. The whites of her eyes were dark red, and her irises were as black as the hallway we were just in, ensuring me that I had no chance of looking away. With her steps approaching me, streams of blood following her the whole way, she remained unflinching as she stared. The others were still franticly looking for an exit as the woman found her way to me, and I immediately began to breathe heavily.

This wasn't scary.

This was *intoxicating.*

I felt a *whoosh* wash through my body at the thought of her instilling fear into me, burning me from the inside out.

The woman reached her hand up to my face, and as if she could read my fascination, she gripped my chin, her bloody skin leaving streaks of the red liquid along my jaw.

That's when the sink turned on, even though no one was near it. Crimson blood sprayed from the faucet on full blast, painting the inside of the sink bright red.

"What the—" Mia whispered.

I tried to turn my head to look, but the bloody woman kept my face in her firm grip, forcing me to keep my eyes on her. Her thumb moved up and trailed my cheekbone, leaving another line of red on my face.

There was a new sensation, a new feeling on my other cheek. I thought she had moved her other hand up to my face as well, but that idea only lasted a second. There was more blood dripping down my skin, but it didn't come from the woman.

It came from above.

Gently lifting my face up, I looked to the ceiling, where I noticed a few sprinkler systems. The one directly above me was coated in red, a new drop growing ready to fall.

"Guys," I began, but as soon as the word left my mouth, there was a *click.*

The sprinkler systems kicked on, but instead of water, they sprayed blood.

Just like the sink.

The white room quickly turned red as the fine mist covered the walls and floor completely. Mia shielded herself with her arms as Elliot ran to her, throwing himself over her in cover.

"Here!" Connor shouted, motioning to a small, hidden door behind the tub. It was only a half door, forcing us to get on our hands and knees and crawl, but it was an exit, nonetheless. As Mia and Elliot went through, Connor came and grabbed my arm, pulling me away from the woman. She didn't move or turn. She only stood in our sudden absence, letting more blood cover her, a grin on her face.

We knew we were heading in the right direction, because in front of us was a red laser. Once we reached that laser, we were able to stand again while our hearts and breathing rushed in a panic. Silent darkness stilled around us as we paused, trying our best to find our bearings.

"What the hell was that?" Mia asked as she panted. "And this is my nice fucking jacket."

I couldn't see her, but through the anger in her voice and the sound of fabric rubbing, I knew she was trying to get a feel for the amount of blood that saturated her clothes.

"Can they do that?" Elliot asked in the darkness. "Ruin our clothes like that?"

"Probably," Connor replied. "Did you read all that fine print before signing?"

He didn't answer, which was an answer in itself.

After a moment of silence and once our breathing began to ease up, I felt Connor's hand rest against my arm.

"Sadie?" He asked, making sure it was me that he was leaning into.

"Hmm?"

"Are you okay?"

"Yeah, I'm good."

Elliot spoke up. "Good. Let's get out of here."

There was a silent agreement between all of us as we continued down the laser-guided path.

"Do you have blood on you?" I asked, leaning closer to Connor.

"A little bit, yeah. I can feel it in my hair."

"Me, too," Elliot replied. "But I think the most of it is on my back."

Mia chimed in. "My sleeves are soaked. But that's pretty much it, I think."

With Connor leading the way, we continued quietly. After a few minutes, I felt his pace beginning to slow, and the rest of us slowed down with him. Then, he stopped completely.

My hands squeezed his arm as I whispered to him, confused. "What's wrong?"

"It's…" Connor started, raising his voice to all of us, and I could hear his hands feeling the path ahead. "The walls. They're… different…"

"Okay…" Elliot let out a chuckle. "So what? Go."

"It feels smaller," Connor replied. "I think."

I reached out to the walls, trying to feel what Connor was referring to. He was right. The width of the hallway felt smaller and shorter than I remember from before. Then again, I couldn't be a fair judge because I wasn't paying much attention.

But what I *did* know was that the walls were no longer made from wood, and they definitely were before. I remember all the hollow *thuds* from the beginning of this house, this maze, whatever we could call it. My palms pressed against the material, trying to get a feel for what it was. Rubber? Latex? Whatever it was, it was tight and didn't have much stretch. I could push on it and it would bend, but it wasn't allowing any more room.

As we went on, the tight walls began to move closer, soon touching our shoulders as we walked.

Then, the walls were *squeezing* our shoulders.

"I don't like this," Mia said behind me, panic in her voice, her breath quickening.

The rubber walls pushed us even more, forcing us to turn and walk sideways until they squeezed against our front and back. I heard Connor grunt, and I knew he was having a hard time pushing through.

"Fuck," he said, his forceful steps slow and his breathing heavy.

We were becoming trapped.

"Are you sure we're going the right way?" Elliot asked from the back. No one answered. How were we supposed to know? The lasers led us here, and they've led us the entire way thus far.

"We need to go back," Mia gasped, the plea loud in her voice.

Maybe she was right. Her nervousness began to creep into my thoughts. What happens if we go in too far and can't get out? Who would help us? Who would hear our screams in the tight, thick rubber? What if this path led us to a dead end, and we were trapped in here, being squeezed to death like a rodent in a snake's coil? With our ribs unable to expand and our lungs unable to draw in a single breath?

What if we suffocated?

As we continued on, the rubber stretched the skin along my face and molded tightly to the rest of my body. I could feel strands of my hair catch on the material, ripping pieces from my scalp out in a yank. My eyes began to water from the annoying, dull pain.

Since we were all walking sideways, I managed to grab the hood of my sweatshirt and shift it up with each step. Thankfully, I was able to slide it up and over my head after a few struggling steps, and now the rubber was no longer ripping out my hair. I pulled the drawstrings and tied them under my chin.

With each step, the rubber walls gripped onto the fabric of my hood, sticking and pulling it off my head. But I kept my hands up, not letting it go, making sure the rubber material was stretching the skin of my hands rather than my hood and hair.

The walls were so tight that they were molding to the shape of my face, and my nose could barely catch an inhale through the small gap my head was making.

Mysterious hands grabbed my ankles, gripping me tight and preventing me from taking another step. I kicked away the hold and stepped forward. Judging by the numerous shouts and curse words behind me, I was betting the others were being grabbed, too.

My breath was hot in my own face, my lips felt like they were being pulled back to my ears, and even though it was still pitch black, my eyes were stretched closed. I could feel the passing heat of Connor's body in the material around me as we took each step.

I felt like I was encased in a balloon that someone sucked all the air out of.

I was wrapped in cling wrap that had no end, no beginning, no openings.

I was stuck in cement that was wet but drying, keeping me in this spot forever.

I was being smothered by a plastic bag over my head, with no room to breathe.

There were no breaks in the path and no offerings of relief.

My head began to spin, my lungs began to shrivel, my throat began to close.

We were suffocating.

Mia must've felt the same way because soon enough, I heard her let out a cry. "I can't breathe."

Another wail came from her tightened chest. It was a short, loud burst, and I knew exactly what was happening.

It was the start of a panic attack.

Her breathing came in light, short spurts, which was the last thing she needed to do in this situation. She needed to breathe steadily and focus, or else getting out of here would be ten times harder.

"Mia," Elliot spoke from the back. "Breathe. We'll be fine."

But it's like his words were caught and sandwiched in the rubber before they could reach her ears. They were silenced in the thickness, and her panic only grew.

"Mia," Connor shouted from the front, his voice loud and booming. "*Mia!*"

Her cries were turning into loud sobs that melted into the compression around her.

Connor yelled again. "Mia, I feel the end."

"You do?" Mia and I both asked at the same time, but her breathing continued at a rapid pace.

"Yeah," he responded and continued pushing through the rubber. "Keep going."

We took another four or five pushes through the rubber, and that's when I realized Connor was lying. He didn't feel the end. If he did, we would've been out by now.

He was telling her that so she would calm down.

My insides warmed at the thoughtfulness. Instead of simply telling her to calm down or chill out, which would have the opposite effect, he gave her the small light at the end of the tunnel that could help her.

And it did.

Mia followed as I pushed through another step, then another, and another. Her panic edged out slowly, but it was clear from her soft, subtle whines that she was still having a hard time. But her tears tapered off, and her breathing settled, if only by a little.

Then, with Connor's feet close to mine, I felt a sudden rush of cool air on my legs. I could hear and feel the ruffling of movement ahead of me as Connor made his way out. Darkness still surrounded my head, but the air was different. It was no longer tight; it was no longer suffocating.

One step forward through an open slit, and that foot was out. Free.

Another step and both of my legs were out. Open. I could move them without any resistance.

The rest of my body fell out of the trap, with Connor catching me on the other side, his grasp on me weak.

Mia and Elliot came through as well, with Mia falling and collapsing on the floor.

"Fuck, what the fuck?" Elliot yelled as he stumbled out, immediately reaching for Mia. He helped her stand back up to her feet as we all tried to catch our breath and right ourselves. It felt like my body was about to liquify into a puddle on the floor.

"Were we just born again? Was that some stupid fucking rebirth?" Elliot shouted, still holding Mia up and gently rubbing her back in circles.

"It's *'The Asylum,'*" I replied while pulling my hood down and meeting Elliot's annoyed stare. "They want us to feel crazy."

Elliot huffed as he held Mia, her weight leaning and slouching onto him. Even though most of my body felt like jelly, some parts of me still felt as if they were being squeezed. My ribs didn't release their tightness even as I tried to take large, deep breaths.

Glancing up to Connor, I was met with his watchful, blue-eyed gaze. Dried blood ran through his light brown hair in streaks, the waves tousled and messy from the tight pressure we had just endured. One curly lock of hair fell over his forehead as he panted, my eyes tracing the softness down to his eyes.

His eyes. His hair.

I could see.

My eyes flicked over to Mia and Elliot, who were still holding each other.

There was light.

We were no longer in darkness, but stood at the end of a long, black-painted hallway with a small window of light halfway down. The bright light from the window shined through and onto the wall across from it. There was also a door next to it with another small window to look through.

As we approached, blood still spotting our clothes and hair and skin, we saw what was inside.

It was an operation room, with two doctors standing over a man lying on a bed. His wrists and ankles were secured in thick belt restraints, clearly struggling in the tight grip. In his mouth was a rubber mouthpiece, his teeth tightly clenched in his muffled screams. Sweat dripped down the sides of his face, past the circular electrodes that stuck to his temples and the wires attached. The veins in his neck looked like they were about to burst through the thin skin, and his shoulders bucked from side to side as he tried his best to resist his pain-filled torture.

"Oh my God," Mia said quietly.

"It's fake, babe," Elliot said reassuringly, even though he didn't sound convinced himself.

But as my heart squeezed and my blood rushed, it didn't look fake. That fear could *not* be faked.

As the doctors continued to try to control the patient, keeping his thrusts and lunges to a minimum, Connor kept walking, looking for a way out. The hallway came to an abrupt stop with a door at the end. He twisted the doorknob, but it didn't budge.

"It's locked."

"What the fuck is this, some sort of escape room?" Elliot asked with a hint of anger.

One of the doctors glanced up at us, peering through the window. His eyes scanned the four of us before speaking.

"One of you, in here. Now."

Mia immediately shook her head. "I'm not going in there."

"Me either," Elliot added.

"*Now!*" The doctor barked. Without hesitation, Connor pulled himself away from the group and opened the door to the hospital room. When he stepped through, the doctor looked at him as he kept his strength on the patient.

"Turn the machine on."

The doctor nodded his head toward the giant silver machine behind him, which had multiple buttons and switches on its front.

Connor studied the machine as his hand hovered over the switches.

"The red one," the doctor said, and Connor eyed it. With a swift flick of his wrist, he lifted the switch, turning the machine on.

The lights flickered, the patient wailed, and the sound of buzzing filled the entire room and hallway. Connor began to step backward, his steps uneasy as he nervously swallowed.

You could almost *see* the vibration of the shock running through the man's body as his eyes rolled back, beads of saliva dripping from his lips.

"That's *not* fake," Mia stuttered, her voice shaken in disbelief.

With the lights continuing to flicker and the machine still running, I heard the door to my left unlock with a *snap*.

"Connor!" I shouted, my eyes still peering through the window as my voice carried through the open hospital door. I quickly motioned for him to come back, and he didn't hesitate before running out of that room and rejoining us. With Connor at my side and the others behind me, I grabbed the doorknob and pushed it open. It led into another dark hallway with one red laser in front of us. Connor stepped up and took the lead again, following the light before another one shined to our left. A few steps to it, and we hit another door.

Connor grabbed the knob, twisted it, and pushed open the door.

The brisk fall air hit me harder than I could've expected as my lungs devoured the clarity.

We were outside.

11:50 PM

THE VISION

"Fuck that," Elliot said after we moved away from the building, out of range from anyone exiting *The Asylum*. "This shit isn't a haunted house. This is some twisted fucking game."

As we did our best to catch our breath and steady our racing heartbeats, we slowly and reluctantly made our way to the next line. I tried to study the faces of the others who finished the first house, the ones who came stumbling out after us. Some were fine, maybe a little shaken, and they walked over and joined the line behind us. Others were outright terrified, turning around as soon as their foot hit the outside ground. They made their way back to the front gate, forgoing any of the other houses. I don't blame them; the experience of the first house was traumatic, and some people simply cannot stomach the whole ordeal.

Oh well. Less wait time for us.

However, the one thing I noticed about everyone leaving the first haunted house was that no one was covered in blood. There wasn't a single red drop on anyone but us. Confused, I tilted my head as I watched a group of girls debate whether they wanted to endure the next house. They looked scared and nervous as they glanced to the second house, but their clothes were dry. They were all clean and put together.

It was as if we experienced a completely different house.

Did we?

Did we experience something different?

Did we take a different path?

"Come on, it wasn't that bad," Connor spoke up, his hands finding his jacket pockets again, his voice snapping me back into our group's conversation.

"Connor," Elliot pressed. "You fucking *electrocuted* a guy."

"Yeah, and that bloody chick grabbed Sadie," Mia added, and the three of them looked at me. Moving my hand up to my face, I tried to wipe the red blood off my skin, but it was already dried on.

"It's fake," Connor said to the others as I continued to rub the blood off. It began to come off in peels, my fingers dusting off the flakes to the ground. "Plus, she wasn't the only one to get bloody."

Mia looked down at her sleeves, which were speckled in red liquid. Connor ran a hand through his hair, breaking up the remaining blood, while Elliot tried to look over his shoulder to the blood on his back. We all had it on us, but it wasn't nearly as much as I had imagined. Maybe most of it came off in the rubber tunnel.

"I didn't think it was *that* bad."

The three looked at me again. Mia and Elliot were surprised by my words, while Conner was the only one to give me a smile.

"Sure, it was intense, but we knew that going in," I added, peeling the last of the blood off my cheek. I looked from Mia, to Elliot, then to Connor, who studied me, almost proud of my fearlessness. "You guys aren't backing out, are you? Because I don't think I'll be able to find another group that will take me in."

"We're not," Connor cut in before anyone else could say anything. Elliot and Mia huddled in close to each other, accepting the fact that I was right. We knew, well ahead of time, that this wasn't a leisurely walk in the park. This was *the* top-rated set of haunted houses in the entire country.

And after a quick wait of fifteen minutes, we were next up to enter *The Vision.*

A guard stood at the door dressed in all black, He held a large cardboard box at his side and a pair of scissors in his hand.

"Bracelet?" he asked, and I raised my wrist. He cut the yellow bracelet, threw away the plastic, and handed me a pair of 3-D glasses. The others did the same behind me, and we all put on the silver glasses before glancing at the door. The guard nodded, allowing us to enter. I stepped in first, with Mia behind me and the two guys behind her.

Pushing a curtain to the side, we entered a long hallway. This time, it was a bright, neon blue with dancing pink lights. I squinted my eyes at the colors. It was a dizzying sight as my eyes and brain adjusted to the contrast through the glasses. I placed both my hands against the walls on each side of me, the pink circles floating in the spaces between, and I swear I could reach out and grab one if I wanted to.

"This is trippy," Mia said behind me, her footing unbalanced with each step.

Leading the way, I walked down the hallway as music blasted in my ears. A heavy dubstep song played, the robotic bass vibrating every inch of my body, finding its way deep into my bones. I kept walking as the lights played with me, sending my body into a tilt. We rounded the corner to another hallway, and this time, the floor was *actually* tilted. I could feel it in the way my heels dug into the ground, trying to catch myself before stumbling. The music continued as I saw more lights added to the ones from before. Purple and bright green dots flickered around the halls in a staggered pattern.

My steps stopped as I looked up at the end of the hallway to see another mounted deer head, the eight points painted a bright, neon pink. I furrowed my eyebrows slightly at the unusual sight. Even though it was painted neon, it didn't fit with the theme of the house.

My heart began to pick up the pace once again. It meant something.

I tucked the image into the back of my mind, my eyes unblinking as I stared at it for a moment too long.

Before the others could catch on to my curiosity, I continued walking. Turning the corner, there was yet another hallway, even brighter than the ones before. There were more lights, more circles, more patterns, more music. The walls were still bright blue, and the purple, green, and pink lights now had orange and white spirals floating around between dancing green lasers. There were so many colors, all of them constantly moving, making it hard to focus. A circular light lined the curved ceiling, causing my mind to think the room was spinning even though it wasn't. I knew that if I took a single step, I would lose my balance and fall right on my ass.

"This shit is giving me a headache," Elliot said from the back.

Cautiously, I took another step forward, and my foot reached an incline. I looked down to the blue floor to see a shiny, reflective surface. Lifting and pressing my foot onto the ramp, I immediately slipped, smacking my knee on the hard floor. My hands braced on the incline before the rest of my body fell, too.

"Shit," I mumbled. I felt Mia grab me, helping me get back to my feet.

Lifting my hands, I looked at my palms. They were slick and slimy, but they were also bubbly.

It was soap.

I looked back to the floor, my gaze following the upward slope, and let out a huff.

"We have to climb this," I tried yelling over the music to the group, but my words were lost in the vibrations of the bass, leaving me no choice but to show them instead of tell them.

I simply knelt back down to my hands and knees. Trying my best, I pressed my hands as hard as possible to the floor, trying to grip anything I could use as leverage. I got *maybe* a half step up before slipping and sliding back down again.

Standing back up, a sickly, sweet scent filled my nose. Bringing my hand to my face, I inhaled. The soap reeked of a sugary scent, something I couldn't put my finger on.

What was that? *Vanilla? Bubblegum?*

No. It smelled like cotton candy.

Even though I had a decent sweet tooth and didn't mind sugary scents, this was overkill. I cringed, and now that it was all over the front side of my jeans, I couldn't get the putrid smell out of my nose.

I looked up to the top, defeat already filling in my chest. It was at least fifteen feet high.

"Mia, give me a push." I mouthed the words and motioned for her to lift me.

I braced myself on my hands and knees, ready to climb. Mia's hands pushed against the backs of my thighs, thrusting me up the slope. Flashing lights still blinded me as I searched for something to hold onto, but there was nothing. I scrambled to stay up, to find a way to stick. By some miracle, the rubber toe of my boot found a dry spot and gripped the floor. Using that foot, I pushed myself up farther, and my hand found the edge of wooden trim against the wall. The tips of my fingers barely latched on, but that's all it took for me to pull myself up. With my feet still slipping out from underneath me and strong scented soap coating the front of my clothes, I made it to the top.

Sure enough, on the ceiling was another deer head, painted bright blue to match the color of the walls. I stared at it, all while lights moved around me, forcing my mind into thinking I was about to fall. I caught myself against the wall and turned around to see the others. Mia was already halfway up, her shoe finding the same dry spot I did, and I reached down to grab her hand and pulled her up with me.

Elliot was next, his larger, heavier frame harder to pull up. His feet slipped a few times, unable to make it past the soap. His legs smacked against the slope, but with Mia and me both reaching and gripping his wrist, we somehow managed to drag him up.

Surprisingly, Connor made it up most of the way by himself, but I still reached my hand out for him. He grabbed my palm and I pulled, bringing his body into mine.

"Thanks," he tried yelling, but since the music was still blasting, my eyes had to glance down at his lips to see what he was saying. His lips curled up in a grin as he watched me through the lights, his glasses making him slightly more attractive. I smirked, but only for a fraction of a second before shaking it off.

With soap covering the front of us, we brushed ourselves off and turned to go down the next hallway, my eyes sparing the deer one final glance. Its beady eyes watched me as I stayed with my group and continued on.

Between the lights, the blasting music, and the sugary smells, it felt like all my senses were working overtime, sending my body into a frenzy.

The walls were still dancing with bright lights, but now they were spinning in deep, delusional circles. I felt like I was hallucinating as I watched the lights spin around me.

And that's when I realized the room was *actually* spinning.

The walls were turning, casting all of us off balance and throwing us onto the floor. But then, as the walls kept moving, we weren't on the floor anymore. With a *thud*, we were lying on the walls. Then, half a second later, we were lying on the ceiling. The room kept turning, the lights kept flashing, the music kept playing, and we kept falling.

"I can't do this," Elliot yelled before taking off his glasses. Just as he ripped them off his face, the room immediately went dark, the walls still tilting through the blackness. Mia, who somehow managed to sit back up, toppled over again after I fell into her.

"I can't see!" Mia shouted as the music continued to play.

"Put your glasses back on!" Connor commanded.

Within a second, the lights switched back on. I glanced at Elliot, who was scrambling on the floor, the glasses back on the bridge of his nose, his hand still on the frame.

The room was still blasted with loud music, but the four of us remained silent as the walls continued to turn. We fell with every twist, our bodies landing with a resounding *thump* each time.

"They're watching us," Connor attempted to shout over the music.

"Who's 'they?'" Mia asked, her voice at the same volume.

No one answered, but we all knew Connor was right. The second we stop playing their game, the game gets harder.

And something about that lit another flame in me.

I already knew that we had to play along, based on the electroshock therapy alone. But to have *actual proof* that we were being watched made me feel carnal. Part of me wanted to take the glasses off just to test my limits and see where it would lead me.

But I didn't think the others would like that, so I played the game the way it was supposed to be played.

We weren't going to make any progress just sitting here in this rotating room, so I pushed myself off the floor and tried to get to my feet. It took me a second to regain my balance, steady my footing, and follow the path of the rotation, but I ended up getting the hang of it. I looked to the far wall, opposite the one we came in, searching for a way out. Thankfully, there was a door, but I had to wait for the correct time to open it. With the lights still flashing in my face, I had to catch it at exactly the right moment.

I walked along the walls, following the path of the spinning room, until the door aligned perfectly along the bottom. I turned the knob and pushed the door open, forcing the room to stop moving. The other three stood to their feet in relief, their steps lopsided as they tried to push away their dizziness.

Looking over my shoulder, I watched them as they followed me, our path leading into another bright hallway. Even through all the different colors, I could see Elliot's face growing pale.

As we proceeded into the next hallway, our pace was slower and more sluggish. Our bodies were taking a toll from the spinning room. Elliot held onto Mia while he closed his eyes, using her as his guide.

But hey, at least his glasses were still on.

The music was even louder, even though I didn't think it could be possible. But with a large speaker in every corner, with every change in direction, the soundwaves rattled the skin on my face and vibrated the floor under us, tickling my feet through my boots.

How they didn't blow out these speakers was beyond me.

After rounding another corner, I ran face-first into something.

Something *solid* but not flat.

Something *black* but not hidden.

Something *firm* but not hard.

Actually, judging by the nudge against my thigh, it was firm *and* hard.

My eyes trailed up, and up, and up.

Until my eyes locked with his.

Before me stood a man, wearing black from head to toe, including a mask that covered his face, minus the eyes. He peered down at me through heavy eyelids, the flashing lights preventing me from seeing the colors of his eyes. My chest felt like it got hit by a truck as I struggled to steady my breath. I took a half step back, accidentally bumping into Connor, who reactively righted me by grabbing my waist. The Man's gaze flickered down to Connor's hands, watching them for a second before moving back up to my eyes.

"Go, Sadie," Elliot barked from the back of the line.

My skin freckled with goosebumps, covering every inch of my body, even though a fresh heat doused me in that moment. My throat felt like it closed completely as my lungs struggled to breathe.

It was him. He was the one who had been watching me. The same stare he's giving me now is the same stare I've been feeling throughout the night. I know that fire. It felt like it was burned onto my skin, the flames stinging every part of me with just one look.

It took me an embarrassing amount of time before Elliot's words registered in my head, and even though my legs felt like cinder blocks, I managed to step around The Man. He didn't move; he simply stood there, his body like a giant roadblock in our quest out of here.

Once out of sight from The Man, I released a deep exhale, ignoring the lights and sounds pressing against me. Connor dropped his hands from my waist once we were in the next hallway. We continued on, the walls relentless in their maze.

At the end, we came upon a gated elevator. It was small, fitting a maximum of four people if we squeezed in enough. The gates were painted neon, matching the theme of the house. With no other choice, I pulled open the gate and we all filed in, our bodies crushed against one another. I looked at the buttons on the inside as Elliot closed the gate. The top button had an up arrow; the bottom button had a down arrow.

"Which one?" I asked, turning my head to the group.

Mia said "down" right as Elliot said "up." They looked at each other in confusion, Elliot growing annoyed at her suggestion.

"Why the hell would we go down? You want to go to a basement? Or a morgue, or some shit?"

"I don't want to be stuck somewhere, El."

Ignoring their bickering, I glanced at Connor, who held my gaze intensely through our glasses. We lingered there for a moment, our newfound assurance in each other making the decision for the rest of us. Reaching around my waist, he tapped the down arrow, which lit up.

With a jolt, the elevator began to descend.

"What the fuck!?" Elliot yelled over the music. Connor looked up to the top of the elevator, ignoring him, with myself and Mia also staying quiet.

In front of us, layers of the building lifted as we were lowered. The ride was only about ten seconds long before it stopped in front of another door. This one was painted black, unlike the rest of the neon building. I yanked open the elevator gate, grabbed the door handle, and flung it open.

We were greeted with the night sky, another food truck, and people talking and laughing.

House number two, complete.

12:12 AM

Racing to the edge of the park, Elliot hunched over a row of bushes, bent at the waist. He began puking up all of his stomach's contents, and I couldn't help but find his sound effects nauseating.

I dropped my 3D glasses into the return box, with Mia and Connor following suit.

"He gets motion sickness," Mia said, vouching for Elliot as he heaved.

I winced at the sound. By the looks of it, with multiple garbage cans and ruffled bushes throughout the back of the house, Elliot wasn't the first one to get sick. I looked over to some picnic tables and benches a few feet over, noticing a few other people sporting queasy-looking faces, their arms clutching the base of their torso. Some people were heading back to the entrance, their stomachs winning the battle, sending them home for the night. The crowd was slowly dwindling with each house.

I turned to Mia and Connor, my gaze volleying back and forth between them before finally settling on the brown-haired guy before me. I tilted my head slightly, my eyebrows slanting down.

"How did you know to go down?" I asked.

Connor smirked. "The soap," he said monotonously. "We went up and never went back down."

I nodded just as Mia spoke up. "I wonder what would've happened if we tried to go up."

"Maybe there was more to the house," Connor said before shrugging. "But I bet the up button didn't even work."

"Yeah, you're probably right."

Elliot coughed after the last of his stomach splayed out on the ground. He wiped the corner of his mouth with his sleeve.

"Fuck," he muttered as he joined the group, his face still stricken with a pale nausea.

"You good?" Connor asked, patting him on the shoulder.

"Yeah, I'm fine. I just need to get some water."

"I'll go with you. Want anything?" Connor turned to me, his hand briefly grasping my elbow to gain my attention. I shook my head before gently pulling away, but he didn't linger long enough to notice. Once the guys were gone, Mia and I slipped into our place in line.

Suddenly, the smell of freshly popped popcorn and pumpkin spice surrounded me, comforting me in a wave of normalcy between the terror-filled houses. Looking around, I saw a few groups of friends snacking on finger foods and sipping on their large drinks. Sporadic horror-themed characters would jump out at those who were unsuspecting. Some people would laugh, others would scream, but everything was all in good fun and high spirits. Chainsaws whirred to life in the distance, but no one seemed to bat an eye at the sound.

I narrowed my eyebrows, my earlier thoughts running back through my head and confusing me once again.

Did we all go through the same houses?

How come some people were terrified and sick to their stomachs while others were completely unfazed?

But then I thought to Connor, and even myself, and realized that fear affected everyone in different ways. Some people had no problem completely blocking everything out, with the ability to separate reality from fiction. Others simply couldn't handle the depths of the imagery, and their minds had no control over the compartmentalization of the things they experienced.

But that was it. *Control.* Some people had it, others didn't. Some people can control what scares them, and even when they *do* feel that fear, they can control their reaction or lack thereof.

When looking in the eye of fear, your reaction is the only thing controlling your fate.

As we stood in line, I held my elbows and noticed the frigid autumn air becoming cooler as the night went on. Even though I wore a sweatshirt, a deep shiver ran down my spine, accompanied by something sharper.

This wasn't from the air.

This felt like something else.

Looking around, I could only see the food truck, benches and picnic tables, the entrance to the next house, and the woods that lined both sides of the park.

There was a crowd, although it was dwindling with each house, and I scanned the faces around me. No one was paying me any mind. Not Mia, who was checking her phone for service. Not even the guys, who had their backs to me as they waited at the food truck.

But as I took one last look over my shoulder, with my hair pulled to the side and my eyes narrowed, I saw him.

The Man I ran into in *The Vision.*

He was standing by the tree line, far away from anyone else.

With his arms by his side, he stood tall, his identity still hidden under a black mask.

But through the mask, his eyes were glued to me.

They were completely unblinking, dark and hooded, filling me with an unknown desire deep in the bottom of my chest. That same river of desire flowed down my entire body, pausing right between my legs before continuing. A new, slick wetness formed in me, and because of my hidden addiction to fear, I didn't even try to stop it.

In fact, I *reveled* in it.

Our eyes remained locked for what seemed like hours before Mia grabbed my attention.

"Earth to Sadie?"

"What?" I asked, finally turning to face her.

"What are you looking at?" she asked before following the path of my gaze. I turned back around, and just like every horror movie known to man, he was gone.

"Sorry," I breathed out, my chest deflating. I faced Mia again, this time with a gentle smile on my lips. "I thought I saw someone I knew."

After a few minutes, the guys came back with four bottles of water, and Connor handed one to me despite my refusal for anything. I took it, and once I opened it and felt the cold water slide down my throat, I was thankful he got it for me.

There was still a decent line ahead of us, so I asked the three of them some questions to kill time.

"How do you guys know each other?" I asked, taking another sip of the water.

"Connor and I have been friends since middle school. We've been through it all, haven't we?" Elliot nudged Connor, who brushed the back of his head with his hand. We all moved forward in the line.

"Yeah, unfortunately, we have." They both laughed before Elliot turned to Mia.

"And I found this one in my junior year of high school," Elliot added, draping his arm around the back of Mia's neck, and she grinned proudly. "Never looked at anyone since."

Connor cleared his throat, his voice coated with disbelief. "I don't know how she's not sick of you yet."

"You mean like how *your* girlfriend isn't sick of *you?*" Elliot asked sarcastically.

I turned to Connor, confused. "You have a girlfriend?"

"No, he doesn't," Elliot answered before Connor could, and he laughed. "That's the point."

Connor shot him a quick look of annoyance before turning to me. Once his eyes were on me, his expression softened, the sight sending an invasive jolt through me.

He lowered his voice to a whisper, leaning closer to me ever so slightly, the sliver of moonlight shining against his eyes.

"If I had a girlfriend, don't you think I'd be leading her through these houses instead of you?"

My heart skipped as I thought back to my hand wrapped around his elbow, walking close to his back in the first house. I clung to him, and I didn't even *know* him.

Heat rushed around my insides as he kept his blue eyes locked onto mine, my cheeks flushing with the realization. His stare dropped down to my lips, only for a fraction of a second before returning to my eyes. I instantly looked away, the subtle intimacy too swift for my liking.

12:22 AM

THE ETERNITY

Soon enough, we were at the front of the line. I looked to the entrance, which was the only part of the house I could see. It was completely covered with trees and foliage, leaving the only hint of a building being the open wooden door a few feet ahead of us.

Another guard stood at the entrance, looking more than bored with his job. He cut each of our green bracelets, throwing the string of plastic away before allowing us entry. Connor didn't even ask if Elliot or Mia wanted to go first since he already knew what they would say.

Connor held his elbow out for me, and I looped my arm through it as we walked through a set of black curtains, the fabric separating in the middle. Mia kept her position behind me, clutching onto my sweatshirt before we even had the chance to see what we were in for.

"Thank God there are no glasses this time," Elliot said from the back.

"Yeah, the last thing we need is you throwing up all over Mia's back," Connor replied, and I snickered behind him. I could practically feel his smile through his body in response to my laugh.

We stepped into a room that was displayed as a living room. There was a beautiful red couch, a coffee table, and a few matching lounge chairs as well. The area was painted with a beautiful maroon, a bookshelf was built into the far wall, and real red roses were in a vase on the table. A lamp in the corner illuminated the space, allowing us to see. Connor stepped forward, eyeing the roses as the rest of us scanned the room.

"This is cute, babe," Mia said to Elliot. "We should decorate our apartment like this."

Elliot didn't respond as he continued to search the room.

There didn't seem to be any significance to this room. Not a jump scare, not a hidden message, not a trick of the eye. Nothing.

Not even a deer head.

We kept going, making our way into the next room. It was a kitchen with gorgeous granite countertops, a gas stove, a sleek steel refrigerator, and a small dining table with chairs. The lights on the ceiling were on but dimmed, as if someone was trying to set some sort of somber mood. It was working because, once again, there was nothing to take note of besides the eerie stillness of the house around us.

"What's the point of this?" Mia whispered in my ear, and I shrugged.

We continued to the next room. It was a bedroom with a large, king-sized bed in the middle of the floor, the wooden headboard pushed against the wall. It was neatly made, with a dark grey comforter and a decent number of pillows placed perfectly at the head of the bed. There were two end tables, one on each side. More roses were placed on both tables, but this time, they were white roses. The room was quiet, the only sound being our footsteps walking across the hardwood.

"Are we just taking a house tour?" Elliot asked, the irritation thick in his words. No one answered, and we simply pressed on.

The next room was clearly an elegant dining room. The first thing that caught my eye was a beautiful crystal chandelier hanging low on the ceiling, completely unlit but shimmering in the darkness. There was a long, rectangular oak table placed in the middle of the floor, and we slowly walked around it. It had a lace runner stretching along the length and place settings at each seat. After looking quickly, I counted twelve settings. Five along both sides and one at each end. The chairs were all pushed in against the table, and I ran a finger along the top of one.

"This is beautiful," I said under my breath, not caring if anyone heard me.

Although the sight of it all was perfect, I couldn't help but feel like I was invading someone's house. There was an unnerving pit in my stomach that I wasn't supposed to be here, like I was sneaking around, like I was violating someone's sacred space. I swallowed the sensation and followed Connor's footsteps as he reached a door and opened it.

We passed the threshold of the dining room only to enter… the living room.

We all did a double take.

It was the same living room as before, the very first room we entered in this house.

And that's when the door behind us slammed shut, causing all four of us to jump, our bodies falling into each other as we turned to look at the door. Mia clutched my arms, and I leaned into her, our breathing fast as we stared at the door we had just walked through.

Elliot reached forward and grabbed the doorknob, but it didn't budge. It was locked.

"What the fuck?" he asked.

I felt Connor grab my arm and pull me away from the door. "Come on," he said, guiding us away. We followed him as he walked past the same red couch, the same chairs, and the same table that held the same roses. We walked out and into the kitchen. It was the same one we already walked through, with the granite and the stove and the fridge and the dimmed lights. The rooms held the same silence, but this time, our steps were heavier and our breathing was louder.

Leaving the kitchen, we found ourselves in the bedroom. King-sized bed. Two end tables. White roses.

All the same.

We didn't even spare anything another glance before slipping out and into the next room, which was the elegant dining room. The chandelier glistened as I studied the same exact plate settings, counting twelve again. Connor stepped up to the door, taking a quick inhale before jolting it open. We walked quickly, trying to peer through the doorframe before stumbling over the threshold.

It was the living room.

And before we could speak a word, before we could breathe another breath, the door behind us slammed.

"What the *fuck!?*" Elliot shouted, anger piercing through his words.

He clearly doesn't seem to do well under pressure.

"I don't understand," Mia spoke with a hint of unease.

Stepping away from me, Connor made his way to the far wall. "There's got to be something…" he began, his words trailing off from thought.

Then, to our right, a woman popped up from one of the red chairs. Her black hair hung over her face, covering her identity as she climbed over the back, toward us. Mia shrieked and tried to grab me, but I caught her instead and pulled her away. Connor reached for me, and we all hustled out of the living room.

Falling into the kitchen, we all panted, our pulses racing at the jump scare.

But here we were, in the kitchen, *again.*

I glanced around, expecting something to be different, but there was nothing. It was all the same.

Same countertops, same stove, same fridge.

I could sense that we were all expecting another jump scare, maybe another woman waiting for us in the corner or behind the fridge. But as we quietly shuffled our feet along, there was nothing. The silence was in our anticipation of *something, anything* to scare us.

With my grip tight on the back of Connor's jacket, his body heat and heavy breathing under my palms, I inhaled deeply while soaking in the feeling of my fear. I thought of the woman in the living room, the guy getting electrocuted in *The Asylum,* the sense of being on the brink of suffocation in the rubber tunnel, and the need to escape the dizziness of *The Vision.* All the images and feelings replayed in my mind and body, and I could feel the giddiness rise inside me, planting seeds I'd come to identify immediately. I knew this feeling, and I knew it well.

I was turned on.

My body was misattributing the adrenaline in my system and flipping switches that weren't supposed to be switched. Even though I knew it was all fake and we were going to find a way out, my body couldn't register it. I couldn't control myself and what was needed for an appropriate reaction. No matter how hard I tried to talk myself down or think like a normal person, it never worked.

I was struggling to enter survival mode. Instead, I was in submissive mode.

We made our way out of the kitchen and into the bedroom, my jeans rubbing against the inside of my thighs, creating friction against my sensitive skin. As much as I enjoyed the feeling, now was not the time. I needed to keep my head on straight.

With my focus back on track, I looked around. Once again, everything was the exact same, down to the white roses on the table.

"I have an idea," Mia whispered to me, but through the silence, the guys could hear her, too. We all paused as she let me go, stepped out of our line, and headed toward the roses. Picking one out of the vase, she eyed the flower momentarily before placing it on the corner of the nightstand.

"If it's still there next time we come around, we know we're walking in circles. If it's back in the vase, we know we're going through a long stretch of fake rooms."

"Good idea," Elliot reassured her as she slid back into her spot in line. I remained quiet. If we were really walking in circles, wouldn't other people be here, too? How were people finding their way out if it was the same four rooms over and over? We surely would've run into someone else at this point.

Connor began walking again, leading the way out of the bedroom and into the dining room.

The dining room was pristine, just like before, and no plate or chair was out of place. Quickly making our way to the door, Connor swung it open, and sure enough, there was the maroon living room again. We all made our way through and turned to look, fully expecting the door to slam.

And it did.

Elliot rolled his head as his shoulders dropped. "This isn't even scary. This is boring."

Ignoring him, we continued through the living room, which no longer had the woman in the chair. She was gone. I searched the corners, around the couch, and even glanced under the coffee table. She wasn't there.

"No jump scares this time," Elliot mumbled.

"That's what they want you to think," Connor replied, keeping his focus on the path ahead.

We found our way into the kitchen, and before we could make our way across, Connor stopped. The room, already barely illuminated, had an added light that was just enough for us to notice. Our eyes followed the light to the fridge, which was open just a crack. Connor walked to it and gripped the handle, opening the stainless-steel door ever so slowly. More light flooded the room as we watched him pull the door open. The inside was completely empty, except for four broken, green bracelets sitting on the shelf inside. Connor reached in and picked one up, pinching it between his fingers.

"Our bracelets?" Mia asked, her voice etched with confusion.

Elliot shook his head. "Those could be anyone's."

I could feel the panic begin to rise in my chest. Elliot was right; they could be anyone's bracelets, but something in me told me they were ours. I couldn't figure out why, but I knew those were the plastic rings around our wrists ten minutes ago.

"Wait," Mia mumbled. She reached out and plucked the bracelet from Connor, studying it before grabbing the other ones resting inside the fridge. Glancing at each one, she picked out one from the four and raised it to eye level.

"Edge's Inferno," she said, turning to us and holding her bracelet up. My mind went back to earlier in the night when we all got our bracelets.

Look, my green one says Edge's Inferno.

It was her bracelet. There was no denying it.

But the last time we saw it, it was being thrown away into a garbage can.

So, how did it end up here?

Connor grabbed all four pieces of plastic from Mia, shoved them in his pocket, and then shut the fridge door, taking the light away with it.

"Come on," he commanded, reaching back to grab my arm and pulling me with him. I could tell he was unnerved, probably thinking the same thoughts as me.

Why were they here? And who put them there?

And how do we get out of here?

The four of us hustled into the bedroom, where our eyes immediately went to the bedside table.

The rose was no longer resting on the edge. It was back in the vase with the others.

I could feel Mia exhale behind me. "See? We aren't going in circles. We just need to keep going, and eventually, we'll find our way out."

No one said anything in response, and I wasn't fully convinced. Something was off about this house, and there were no words I could find and use to describe the feeling I had.

"Or," Elliot spoke up, taking me by surprise. "Maybe that chick from the living room is following us and fucking with our heads. She could've put the rose back."

It was a legitimate thought. Maybe there were others hiding in the shadows, under the bed, in the cupboards, waiting for us to move along before changing the scene. Right now, I wasn't sure what to think.

"Just go," I whispered to Connor's back, and he turned his head to listen to my words over his shoulder. Without hesitation, he continued on, and we all followed.

But when we entered the dining room, we all stopped dead in our tracks.

In front of us were the twelve chairs, all from the elegant table set, pinned upside down on the ceiling. Mia gasped at the sight, flinging herself onto Elliot, who pulled her in close.

"There's no *fucking way* that girl could've put these up there," Mia whisper-shouted through her sudden loss of breath.

And she was right. There were either more people in on this, or we were walking through a long stretch of hallway with hundreds of duplicate rooms. But that didn't explain how nothing changed in the actual layout. In order for it to *not* be a continuous circle, there would have to be a change. An inconsistency. The walls would have to become a different shape, to warp into something that would allow us to move into another path. We were not walking upwards or downwards or on any sort of slope, at least not that I noticed. The sizes of the rooms were unchanging, and the direction of our path was consistent.

We were walking in circles.

I think.

"Elliot," Connor began, finally tearing his eyes away from the chairs on the ceiling.

The three of us met his stare as he lit up with another idea.

Motioning to the door ahead, he spoke clearly. "Do *not* let this door close. Keep your foot in it."

"Me? Why me?" Elliot protested, but we all ignored him.

Connor ripped open the door, only for it to take us back into the living room. From what I could see, everything was the same. One by one, we stepped through, and Elliot hesitantly made his way over the threshold. Before he could step all the way in, he turned and placed his foot on the side of the doorframe. The door moved to slam closed but bounced back off the rubber of Elliot's shoe. Then, it tried to slam again, catching Elliot off guard, but fell open once more. The door continued its efforts to close but never did.

Connor tugged on my arm. "Let's go."

Reaching back, I grabbed Mia's sleeve, pulling her along with me.

"I'm not leaving him," she yelled to me as she looked back at Elliot.

"You're not. He'll catch up to us."

With an inward groan and a nod from Elliot, Mia followed. We raced past the kitchen, through the bedroom, and into the dining room. With an immediate halt, Connor held his arms out, holding me and Mia back. My heart continued to race, and my blood kept its heated flow as I looked to the scene in front of me.

The chairs were back to normal, all sitting perfectly on the floor.

But now, as I looked up toward the ceiling, instead of a beautiful crystal chandelier, it was a chandelier made of dozens of antlers.

Deer antlers.

I swallowed the lump in my throat, forcing any fear I had down with it.

"Elliot?" Mia asked, pushing past me and heading to the door.

It was completely closed. No shoe, no bounce back, no opening.

Slamming her palm on the wood, she spoke through the door. "Elliot, this isn't funny."

Without a second thought, Mia twisted the doorknob and pushed her way in. She peeked behind the door, expecting him to jump out and scare us. But he didn't. The room was silent.

My eyes instantly moved to her hand, the hand that was slowly letting go of the doorknob, and I screamed.

"Mia, *no!*"

But it was too late. Connor and I both ran to the door right as it slammed shut, our hands pounding on the wood. I tried jiggling the doorknob, but it was already locked.

"Mia!" I shouted. "Mia, are you okay?"

But the only thing on the other side of the door was silence. My breathing began to quicken, with my arousal intensifying at the same pace as my pure fear. It was meant to be all fun and games, but when you were *actually* stuck with absolutely no way out, the fun seemed to quickly turn to dread. I could feel the panic weighing on my chest, growing heavier with each passing moment.

"Shit. *Shit!*" Connor ran his hands through the waves of his hair. "I need to get Elliot."

He turned to run back in the direction we came, and I followed.

"I'm going with you."

As he spared me a satisfied glance over his shoulder, he took me back out of the dining room, through the bedroom and kitchen, and into the living room.

And the second we stepped into the living room, my knees almost gave out as we both struggled to breathe.

Before us was *not* Elliot, like we were expecting.

Before us was Mia.

She was trying to open the door, with both hands pulling the knob, her weight leaning back with everything she had.

"What the *fuck?*" Connor choked out, and my disbelief was right there with him.

Mia instantly turned around at our voices, and judging by the sudden paleness, she wasn't expecting us on this side of the door either.

"Oh my God," she ran to us, falling between us in fear. Connor and I grabbed her, keeping her on her feet as she shook with nerves. "How did you—where's Elliot?"

The lack of an answer from either one of us said everything Mia needed to know. Her spine straightened, and her fear turned to anger. She looked away from us and back to the door. With one final grab, she tried to open it, but it was still locked. Frustrated, she pushed past us and walked out of the living room, through the empty kitchen and bedroom, Connor and I following closely behind. When we got to the dining room, everything was still the same, and Elliot was still nowhere to be found.

Mia ripped the door open, and we had no choice but to follow her unless we wanted to be separated again.

Elliot was not there.

We walked through the circle two more times, both with unchanging results. We entered the living room, and the door slammed behind us.

Mia turned around and tried to open the locked door but failed. I watched her with wide eyes as she dropped her shoulders, her breathing fast and her panic leaking out of every pore in her skin. Without warning, she let out a deep groan, one that festered from the depths of her soul as insanity slowly consumed her from the inside out. The groan turned to a yell, then a shriek, before settling on a toe-curling scream. I could feel Connor tense under my grip.

"Elliot!" she screamed at the door in front of her. "Where the *fuck* are you?"

Her face turned a bright red from the force of her screams.

There had to be something we were missing. We needed to find a shift in the repetition. The bracelets were a clue, a hint to a change.

But there had to be more.

Letting go of Connor, I turned and ran to the red couches against the wall. I pulled off all the cushions and pillows, tossing them over my shoulder.

There was nothing to find.

I did the same with the lounge chairs.

Nothing.

I moved to the bookshelf behind me. I began ripping the books from the shelves, letting them fall to the floor without a single glance down.

"Sadie! What are you doing?" Connor shouted to me, and Mia turned to see what I was up to.

"We're missing something," I said my thoughts out loud, not bothering to stop.

Book after book fell from the shelves, some opening as they landed, the pages creasing under the weight of the hardcovers. I made my way from top to bottom, and when I got to the shelf on the floor, a hint of something caught my eye. Falling to my hands and knees, I flung the remaining books away and reached back, grabbing something long and round.

It was a wooden baseball bat.

"What—" Connor began, but before he could finish his question, I lifted the bat over my shoulder and swung at the bookshelf, creating a crack along the side of the frame.

"Holy shit!" Connor exclaimed.

"Sadie!" Mia panicked and approached me, grabbing the bat before I could swing again. "Are you crazy? That's vandalism! What are you doing?"

"Playing their game."

Pulling the bat away from Mia, I turned to the coffee table, lifted it over my head, and slammed it down. The wood cracked in half, causing the table to fall into a V shape, with jagged pieces running down the middle. I raised the bat again and smashed it down onto the vase of roses, causing glass to shatter under the blunt force. Small, sharp pieces scattered everywhere, and water splashed onto the floor, forcing Connor and Mia to take a step back. Slamming the table a few more times, I broke out in a small sweat, losing my breath in the process.

After the table was crumbled to pieces, the wood sharp and splintering, I studied the ground for any sort of clue I may have missed.

There was nothing but broken furniture and thrown pillows.

I looked over my shoulder to the others. Mia looked concerned, probably fearing we would end up getting kicked out, and Connor looked proud, like he couldn't believe I just did that.

"Who's next?" I asked, showing off a sleek smile and holding out the bat.

"Hell yeah," Connor said, grabbing the bat from me. With slow steps, he made his way past me and into the kitchen. From what we could both see, there wasn't much to break. I did a once-over of the stove, fridge, and cabinets to see if there was anything we may have missed, but there was nothing. Mia followed close behind me, her frustration for Elliot still seething through her pores.

With the bat tight in his fist, Connor made his way into the bedroom. With one look at the furniture, a devilish grin appeared on his lips. He glanced back to me, sending me a wink before squaring up and settling the bat over his shoulder. Mia and I hovered in the doorway, and I could feel her lean over toward me.

"Did he forget to mention he's a baseball player?" Mia whispered with a coy smile.

Before I could respond, Connor approached the first nightstand, swung the bat, and smashed the vase of white roses. His swing was perfect: his elbows were straight, he stepped into the momentum, and his follow-through was smooth as silk. Glass shattered into hundreds of little pieces while white rose petals flew into the air. Mia and I held up our arms and shielded ourselves, even though we were far enough away from the damage. The nightstand tipped over, and water spilled onto the floor. Connor stepped around the bed, walked to the other nightstand, and smashed the other vase.

More glass, more water, more rose petals.

But this time, when the vase shattered, a light *clink* hit the floor.

That *wasn't* glass.

Connor must've heard it because the second the sound rang through the room, he instantly dropped the bat and searched the floor. Within seconds, he moved to grab something, then stood back up.

In his hand was a key.

Mia gasped. "That must've been in the vase."

Connor and I locked eyes, knowing this was the missing piece we needed.

Leaving the bedside, Connor ran to us and led the way out. We entered the dining room, where the table was still neatly set and the antler chandelier was lit.

But now, we had a guest.

Sitting in the middle seat along the far side of the table, with his covered forearms propped against the edge, was The Man. Immediately, I stopped in my tracks, causing Mia to run into my back.

The Man watched my chest as I breathed heavily, his bold stare penetrating the darkest parts of me.

Even with the light of the chandelier above, I couldn't see anything except his eyes.

And they were *heated*.

"Sadie," Mia said behind me, giving me a slight shove. My shoulders thrust forward, but my feet remained planted on the ground. Connor was already at the door, fumbling with a new lock that wasn't on *any* of the previous doors.

"It's still locked," he said to us. "The key doesn't work."

"Sadie," Mia spoke again, this time harsher.

I ignored her and kept my eyes on The Man. "Connor," I said, and he turned to look at me, finally registering what was happening. His eyes volleyed between me and The Man before he slowly came back to my side.

"The bracelets," I began. "Do you still have them?"

He reached into his jacket pocket, pulled out the four green bracelets, and placed them into my outstretched palm. Both Mia and Connor watched me as I gripped the plastic and stepped up to the table. The Man's eyes followed me, trailing my every move, keeping me tight in his vision.

Leaning forward, I reached over to the plate in front of him and dropped the bracelets, the soft *tinks* the only sound in the room. His hands were so close to mine, I could almost feel his body heat. Part of me expected him to quickly reach out and grab my wrist, to scare me, to take me away from anyone and anything.

But he didn't.

I stepped back from the table, my chest heaving, my eyes unblinking.

And that's when we heard a click of the door.

Mia and Connor both looked at the sound. Connor ran to the lock, key in hand, and pushed it in. With a quick turn of the wrist, the door unlocked and swung open. I could feel the bitter rush of nighttime air on my side, but my stare remained on The Man.

"Elliot!" Mia shouted, and I could hear her frantic footsteps take her outside.

Connor stayed by the door, refusing to let go of the handle. "Sadie, let's go."

I swallowed a lump in my throat, and The Man's eyes dropped down to my neck, watching the motion. I was frozen. Something kept me here, attached to the person who had been watching me, following me, studying me. I felt paralyzed under his gaze.

"Sadie!"

A warm presence pressed against my side, and I didn't have to look to know it was Connor. He began to pull me away, forcing me to snap out of my trance. His hand moved to the small of my back, his gentle touch escorting me to the finish line. Elliot held the door open as I walked over the threshold that led to the outside rather than into another living room.

We did it. We made it out.

We escaped the house that defied all reason.

And I could feel the heat of The Man's stare on Connor's hand the whole way.

1:11 AM

"It doesn't make sense," Mia said, confused. "How was that possible?"

The four of us stood outside of *The Eternity*, completely stumped as to how the house operated. We stared at the door, the one we all just came out of, and the building around it. It was small, way smaller than what we just experienced.

"There's no way we spent forty-five minutes in a house *that* tiny."

Mia was right. From the back, it looked like a shed. Maybe a small barn or an extremely small townhouse, but even that was being too generous. No explanation could justify the numerous laps we did, the endless circling we walked, all for us to exit a *shack*.

"What the hell happened to you?" Connor asked Elliot, who seemed calm and collected.

"Nothing, really. I got tired of waiting for you guys, so I let the door close behind me." He shrugged. "I walked through the rooms until I got to the dining room door, opened it, and it led me outside."

My head was spinning at the thought. How could Elliot walk through the house without seeing us, without crossing our path, without needing a key, or without seeing broken glass everywhere?

This wasn't a haunted house.

This wasn't fear.

This was confusion.

This was a complete *mindfuck*.

I could only imagine the groups of people who could never find their way out. What happens to them? How do they end up leaving? Looking around, I only spotted a handful of groups walking throughout the park. How did we dwindle down to this? Did people leave on their own accord, or did everyone get lost?

"You mean you didn't need a key?" Mia asked Elliot, her grip tight on his arm.

Elliot shook his head.

It didn't make sense.

But then again, sometimes fear isn't a quick adrenaline rush. It doesn't have to be a jump scare, blood, or serial killers. Fear can be in the darkness of the unknown, the inability to find an escape, or the anxiety of confinement.

Fear can be forced restlessness.

Fear can be insanity.

No one else had anything to say. We were all confused, distraught, and conflicted. There was no use trying to figure it out because there was no logical explanation for it. There were no answers.

As we made our way to the fourth house, Mia paused.

"Hey," she began with a slight quiver in her voice. "I think I might sit this one out."

My head snapped in her direction, and my eyes widened. "What? Why?"

She brought her arms up to her chest, her hands rubbing her sleeves. It was clear the last house—all the houses, actually—had taken a toll on her. Her face was still pale, and her breathing was still quick. My heart dropped just an inch.

"I just… I don't know. That last one took a lot out of me."

Elliot wrapped his arm around her shoulders to soothe her, and I stepped closer to her.

"Are you okay? Do you need water or anything?"

She shook her head. "No, I'm fine. I just don't want that to happen again."

"What to happen?"

"I don't want us to get separated."

I sighed. "Mia, it's a haunted house. It's not real. Even if we do get separated, no one gets hurt." I motioned to Elliot. "He wasn't with us, and he turned out fine."

"Eh, debatable," Connor chimed in with a laugh.

I smirked over my shoulder to him, playfully swatting him with the back of my hand.

Elliot pulled Mia in close to his chest. "If you don't want to go, I'll hang back with you."

A wave of dread washed over me. Normally, I'd be fine with that idea, but after encountering The Man in the last house, I felt safer in a bigger group. I didn't want to put myself or Connor in a position where one of us would have to face him alone.

"Mia," I whispered, trying to give it one last shot. "Listen. Why don't you guys just try one more? If you don't want to do the last one, we don't have to. We can call it a night. Hell, if you want out in the middle of this one, I'll find a way to get you out."

I could see the contemplation on Mia's face as she ran through her thoughts. Bringing my hands to my face, I made silent prayer hands, pleading with her to give it one final chance.

"Come on," I pushed. "Girls stick together."

A small smirk formed on Mia's lips at the statement.

"Fine," she said, and I smiled. "But if I hate it, I'm not doing the last one."

"Deal!" I shrieked, looping my arm through hers. "Thank you," I said in a whisper only she could hear. She gave me a light squeeze on my elbow, acknowledging my gratitude.

The four of us stepped in line for the fourth house, *The Cloud*. There were only two groups in front of us, but the wait between entering was longer than usual.

"So, you play baseball?" I asked Connor, turning my body toward him.

He nodded, and to my surprise, he turned a bit bashful as he slid his hands into his jacket pockets.

Bumping my elbow against his, I smiled. "How good are you?"

Judging by his perfect swing, I knew he had to have played more than just recreationally.

He shrugged. "I played little league ever since I could hold a bat, and I played for my middle school, too. Then," he paused, glancing down to the ground. "I played for my high school. I was starting pitcher."

I raised my eyebrows. "Wow. That's amazing."

He cleared his throat with a grin. "And then I played for the Florida Gators all four years of college. It was the most incredible time in my life. I felt like I was on top of the world."

I could see the pride on his face and hear the passion in his voice. It warmed my heart to hear someone be so enthusiastic about something they loved.

"I was in talks to be drafted to the minor leagues." His voice dropped as he rubbed his jaw. "But then I fucked up my elbow. I had to get Tommy John surgery, and it just hasn't been the same since."

My expression faded as the subject moved in a somber direction, the ambience around us turning cold like the midnight air. From what he was telling me, to the hurt look on his face, it seemed like a sore subject.

"Now, I work for a fucking *insurance agency*. I could be out on the field, doing what I love, but I wore myself out too early."

There was a long pause before I frowned. "I'm sorry, Connor. That's unfair."

Connor brushed it off quickly with a roll of his shoulders. "Nah, it's all good." His friendly eyes met mine. "Picking up that bat in there, though, felt amazing." He gave me a perfect white smile, and I almost melted right there. The way his blood-tinted hair fell right over his eyes, the way his posture stayed firm, and the way his gaze held mine all played into the thrill of the night.

I sent him a hint of a smirk back and glanced to the front of the line. We were almost there.

I found myself thankful that Mia took me under her wing at the beginning of the night. The three of them were so friendly, so welcoming, and I felt like I was meant to meet them.

But I also knew that *someone else* didn't feel the same way.

1:25 AM

THE CLOUD

Each of us raised our wrists to the security guard, allowing him to cut the red bracelet off. I watched as he threw each piece of plastic into a nearby trash can and wondered if those would find our way back to us like they did in the last house.

Connor stepped forward, not sparing a glance at any of us before leading the way. The building in front of us was long and thin, almost looking like a miniature shopping plaza. The entrance was located at one end where we faced a blank, black door. Connor opened it, and we stepped inside.

Immediately, we were blinded by a bright light, but our vision was clouded by a hazy substance. Elliot and Mia coughed behind me, their lungs trying to expel whatever we were inhaling. I waved a hand in front of my face as I tried to clear some of the artificial fog away, but it was impossible. There was so much of it completely surrounding every inch of us. I couldn't see any part of Connor even though my hand was still gripping his sleeve.

"I can't see a damn thing," Elliot said with a cough.

"I think that's the point," Connor replied through the vapor.

Lights continued to blind us as they reflected off the haze, making it even harder to navigate. It was like driving at night through heavy fog with your high beams on. It probably would've been easier to go through this house in complete darkness.

Shielding my eyes with my free hand, I followed Connor as he walked. There were a few moments when he would accidentally step into a wall, or some sort of other dead end, but for the most part, he found his way around.

"There's a fence next to us," he said, and I immediately stuck my hand out to the right. There was a chain link fence, and I assumed it was there to help guide us, like the lasers in *The Asylum*.

The four of us kept our hands on the fence, our palms continuing to glide along the metal and our fingers dipping in the gaps. We kept our focus, we stayed in line, and we kept calm. So far, the only thing scary about this house was our inability to see and our struggle to openly breathe.

We rounded a few corners, walked along some hallways, and found our way through a clouded maze. It seemed to go on for a long time, with no breaks in the fog, no jump scares, and no music or sounds to distract us.

Then suddenly, Connor stopped, causing me to run into his back. I could feel his body move hesitantly as his shoulders leaned back toward me, but he wasn't stepping forward. We were at a standstill.

"What's wrong?" I whispered as his head neared mine, my breath warm on his neck.

"There's something…"

I waited for him to finish as his body continued to move in a shimmy.

"There's something blocking the path."

"What, like a door?"

"No," he said, and I could feel his body turn to face mine. He leaned in close to my ear. "It feels like a person lying on the ground."

Moving to look over Connor's shoulder, I did my best to try to see through the fog and find what he was referring to, but I couldn't. All I could see was a white, blinding vapor.

"Can you go around them?"

"No. There's no room. There's a wall on one side and the fence on the other."

"Can you step over them?"

Before he could answer, Elliot shouted from the back of the line. "What's going on?"

Connor sighed before speaking to all of us, his voice back to normal volume. "You're going to have to walk over something."

"Okay?" Elliot replied with either frustration or annoyance. I couldn't tell without looking. Probably both. "Just go."

Connor turned back around, away from the group, and began to step over. While still holding onto him, I could feel him shift his weight forward, then completely fall. I tried to catch his arm, but it slipped out of my grasp.

"Connor?" I shouted.

"Ah, fuck," I heard his voice through the fog, and I knew he was only a few feet in front of me. After trying to waft away some vapor but failing, I reached for him, for his hand, anything. I shuffled forward only to kick something—or someone—on the ground.

"Did I kick you?" I asked, my palms still searching for Connor.

"No. That wasn't me."

I swallowed. I know my foot touched *something*. Lifting the toe of my boot, I felt around the ground, making contact with whatever was there once again.

"Sadie," Connor grunted, and soon, I felt his familiar hands grab mine in guidance. "I'm here." Gently, he pulled me forward, and I would've tripped over the person on the floor if Connor wasn't there to steady me.

With a voice loud enough for all of us to hear, he spoke. "There's more than one of them."

My eyes aimed toward the ground as I tried to peer through the haze, but it was too dense for me to see through.

"They're body to body. We have to walk on them."

"*What?*" Mia shrieked in disbelief.

"Are you sure we're going the right way?" I asked.

"Yeah," Connor began, although he didn't sound too convinced himself. "I felt the walls the entire time. There's no other way to go."

We all paused for a few moments, unsure whether to go forward or not. This felt weird, this felt odd. What kind of sick haunted house made you walk on human bodies? What if we stepped on someone's face or throat? What if we accidentally cracked one of their ribs?

What if these people weren't actors?

I shook the thought away and nodded, even though no one could see me.

"Let's just get this over with."

I felt Connor turn, his hands keeping mine in a tight grip. I stepped up on the first person, expecting some sort of groan or grunt, but there were no sounds. My feet were unsteady as I walked across a few bodies, feeling all kinds of mounds and bones and rolls underneath my shoes.

"How many are there?" I heard Mia ask behind me, her hands still holding my sweatshirt.

"I don't know," I replied. I tried to count, but since everyone was body to body, I couldn't tell where one person began and another one ended. I could tell some were lying left to right while others were lying right to left, and some were face down while others were face up. Through the rubber sole on my boot, I could feel one person's spine crack from top to bottom as I walked on their back, but there were still no noises from any of them.

Finally, I felt Connor stumble downward onto stable ground. He let out a heavy breath as he helped guide me.

Before any of us could speak, Mia let out a bloodcurdling scream.

"*My ankle!*"

"What the *fuck?*" Elliot yelled from the back of the group. I quickly turned to find Mia.

"Someone has my ankle!"

Losing her balance, Mia toppled forward onto my arms. I tried to keep her upright, but her momentum was too strong, and she fell onto the last few bodies. Both Connor and I reached our arms out to find her, grab her, and pull her away.

"Get *the fuck* off of me!" she screamed. My hands made contact with her shoulders, and I could feel her thrashing body try to kick whatever had a hold on her.

"Please, *help me,*" a trembling, soft voice came from the ground. "Please."

Mia screamed again, this time with a hint of a cry.

"Motherfucker!" Elliot shouted. I could hear slight shuffling but still couldn't see a thing.

"Please, *save me.* Help." This voice was different from the first one, making my skin crawl.

"Get off!" Mia yelled through clenched teeth, then released another cry. "Oh, God, there's more of them."

"Help."

"Please, help me."

A deep, hoarse voice boomed over the others. *"Save me."*

More voices came from the depths of the ground, all begging and pleading for safety. Mia turned her shoulders to me, and I grabbed her elbows right as she grabbed mine. There were more hands along her arms, swallowing her, running their slimy, cold fingers along her jacket and onto my hands as well. I had to resist every urge to shake them away and take off running. I could feel Connor come in close to me, and somehow, he managed to squeeze his way through the lake of hands, slip his arms under her, and lift her away from the remaining bodies. Elliot pulled whatever—or whoever—off of Mia's ankles, legs, torso, and arms, whipping them all away from her while fighting off their grips on him as well. With all our might, Connor and I pulled her to the cold ground, and Elliot stumbled onto us only seconds later. We all sat on the hard floor, our breathing ragged as the fog continued to surround us.

"Is everyone okay?" I asked quietly.

"No," Mia immediately answered hastily.

"Mia—"

"Fuck this. I'm getting out of here."

I could hear her stand to her feet, with Elliot following suit. The fence *clinked,* and I knew her hand was trailing along as she resumed the path. Without saying a word, Connor stood up, pulling me with him. He settled behind me as I eased in behind Elliot. We all continued on in silence.

Aside from a cough here and there, no one said anything. I could sense Mia's anger, even with Elliot between us. After more twists and turns, Mia stopped.

"There's a door," she said quietly, as if she didn't want to speak to us anymore.

"Is it unlocked?" Connor asked from the back.

There was a pause before we heard the twist of the handle, then the opening of the door.

Still unable to see in front of me, I asked, "What is it?"

Mia stuttered before answering. "I'm… I'm not… I'm not going in there first."

Connor passed me, Elliot, and Mia, and took his place at the front of the line. A wave of unease washed over my back, and suddenly, I missed having someone behind me, guarding me. I felt exposed. I turned my head to look over my shoulder to see if there was someone, *anyone* there, but my efforts were futile in the dense fog.

But with the way the night was going, I'm sure we weren't alone.

Without warning, we began to shuffle along, and I instinctively grabbed onto Elliot's jacket. Our footsteps were light and quick, careful not to trip or misstep. The door closed behind us as we entered the new room, only to come into nothing. There was no fog, no blinding lights, no fence.

Nothing.

Our steps took us down a slight slope, and I used Elliot to keep my balance as we trailed along. I blinked a few times, trying to help my eyes adjust to the blackness, but there was no use. There was no light for my vision to cling to, to absorb, to dilate on. Finally, after descending, we stood on level ground. Connor stopped.

"I don't know where to go," he said in the darkness, his voice echoing in the vast space around us.

I could feel the beat of my heart speed up at the unknown.

The unknown of what comes next.

The unknown of what's around me.

The unknown of the way out.

I could feel my blood pulsing, my heartbeat in my ears, and the slickness between my legs.

"Should we try to find—"

Before Elliot could finish his question, four spotlights switched on from the ceiling above. We all shielded our eyes at the sudden contrast, our pupils confused at the constant switching. The lights shined down onto four separate podiums, each spaced about six or seven feet apart. Moments later, along the wall in front of the podiums, a giant screen turned on. TV static played on the screen for a few seconds as we all turned to face it. Then, a message came on, with a black background and white letters.

STEP UP TO YOUR OWN PODIUM

We all shot a glance to one another before reluctantly moving forward. Connor took the podium farthest to the left. I chose the spot next to him as Mia settled in to my right, with Elliot standing at the other end. I was surprised Mia didn't put up a fight, but I didn't dare say anything. Just like when Elliot took off his 3D glasses, if Mia didn't play along, things would probably be more challenging for all of us.

As we were illuminated by the warm lights above, we glanced at each other nervously.

The words flashed away, leaving only a blank black screen before a new message appeared.

YOU MUST ALL ANSWER THE QUESTIONS
CORRECTLY WITHIN THE ALLOTED TIME. USE THE
SCREEN IN FRONT OF YOU TO CHOOSE YOUR ANSWER.

I looked down to the podium before me. There was a screen, about the size of a small tablet, planted inside the surface. I ran my hand over it, feeling the smoothness of the glass. The screen powered on, and a blank white square lit up under my palm.

I looked back up to the directions on the wall.

DO NOT BE INCORRECT

The sound of Mia's sharp inhale forced me to turn and look at her. Her face was as white as a ghost, and her eyes were wide with fear.

"Mia," I whispered, and it came out as more of a hiss. "Mia, look at me."

With a tremble, she did.

"It's going to be fine. We can do this. It's not real, remember?"

She shook her head as her eyes turned glossy, and in that moment, I knew this was the end. There was no way she was going to go into the final house, if she could even manage to pull through this one.

I looked over to Connor, hoping for reassurance, but his eyes were still glued to the screen ahead.

There was a quick beep, and my head snapped back to the instructions, where there was now a countdown.

3… 2… 1…

I swallowed a nervous lump in my throat as a question appeared.

$$2 + 2 = \underline{}$$

A countdown began, starting at *10.*

9… 8… 7…

The screens on our podiums flashed, and I looked down to see four different squares, each holding a number that we could tap and select.

Without hesitation, I tapped the square in the bottom left corner.

4.

Out of the corner of my eyes, I saw the others do the same. I glanced back up to the screen, where the countdown continued.

3… 2… 1…

The simple math equation vanished, leaving another blank, black screen. Then, one word appeared.

CORRECT

No one said anything as we all kept our eyes on the screen, and I found myself fearing the idea of answering a question incorrectly. What would happen?

Before I could dwell on the thought, a new question appeared in the same bold, white letters.

HOW MANY SIDES DOES A TRIANGLE HAVE

10… 9… 8…

The screen in front of me lit up with another set of choices. I immediately tapped the first box, which held the number *3*.

The others did the same. The timer continued to tick down when Connor turned, leaning forward to yell over at Elliot.

"Hey, the answer is three if you didn't know."

Elliot narrowed his eyes. "Fuck you."

Mia and I couldn't help but snort and laugh. The question disappeared as the time ran out, and our results appeared.

CORRECT

I exhaled. This was suspiciously easy. I knew there had to be a catch at some point.

Another question appeared.

WHO CREATED THE FAMOUS PAINTING, "THE LAST SUPPER"

10...9...8...

Four squares popped up on the screen in front of me. I looked through the choices.

VINCENT VAN GOGH
PABLO PICASSO
SALVADOR DALI
LEONARDO DA VINCI

"It's Van Gogh, right?" Mia asked, turning to look at me, then at Elliot, who shrugged.

I shook my head. "It's Da Vinci."

"Are you sure?" she asked, and I could feel everyone's stares on me.

5...4...3...

I nodded, and everyone tapped their answer.

2...1...

CORRECT

I released an exhale. With my palms turning clammy and my forehead beginning to sweat, I knew this was only going to get more complicated.

There was no time to steady my nerves before the next question presented itself.

HOW MANY STARS ARE ON THE AUSTRALIAN FLAG

10...9...8...

"*Fuck*," Elliot shouted, and I instantly knew that tone. It was defeat.

There were four options to choose from, but none of them were sticking out to me. I tried to close my eyes and picture the flag, but I couldn't even place a color.

I looked at the choices again.

2

6

10

30

"It's gotta be ten, right?" Connor asked.

"I have no fucking clue," Elliot replied.

Mia chimed in. "I think it's six."

5...4...3...

"Quick, just pick one." My voice was quivering as my fingers hovered over the screen, trembling. I tapped the number 6 and instantly looked up at the timer.

1...

The screen went black, and I held my breath. Seconds that felt like minutes passed before a word appeared.

INCORRECT

My heart dropped to my feet as I glanced to Connor. "What did you press?"

"Six."

I looked to Mia, who was firmly gripping the podium, her knuckles a bright shade of white. "I picked six, too."

The three of us looked to Elliot, who opened his arms wide. "What the *fuck*, guys? Why didn't you tell me we were deciding on six?"

Before any of us could answer him, the floor underneath him gave way. He fell through a dark, open square, the new void swallowing him whole in half a second. Once he was completely gone, the door in the floor closed as if it had never even opened.

"Elliot!" Mia screamed. She ran over to his spot and fell to her knees. With hard, heavy fists, she slammed on the trap door, wishing for it to open again.

My stomach dropped, my pulse accelerated, and I could feel my adrenaline start to kick up. I turned to look at Connor, who looked just as freaked out as I did. Mia was continuing to slam her hands on the trap door when a new question appeared on the screen.

"Mia," I hissed. "Get up. There's more."

Ignoring me, she yelled for Elliot again. Tearing my eyes away from her, I looked up to the new question.

IN THE GAME OF CHESS, THE BISHOP MOVES IN WHICH DIRECTION

"Diagonal," Connor shouted before the answers appeared on our screens, and I didn't even question it. Once they popped up, I pressed the correct button, then ran to Mia's podium and did the same. She was still kneeling on the floor, but now she was digging her nails into the crevices of the door, doing everything in her power to make it open.

"Mia," I spoke gently as the timer on the screen counted down. "Mia, he's fine. He's probably waiting for us outside like he was in the last house."

Mia paused to look at me over her shoulder. A flash of annoyance crossed over her face before softening. "How do you know?"

I shrugged. "It's just a haunted house."

There was a second of hesitation before she completely turned herself toward me, still sitting on the floor. She looked as if she didn't want to give in to me or admit I was right. She stayed on the floor for a moment, pausing to wipe her nose on her sleeve and catch her breath. She didn't make eye contact with me.

The screen illuminated with our result.

CORRECT

I held my hand out to Mia, who reluctantly took it with trembling fingers. I helped her stand to her feet as we made our way back to our spots. I could hear her breathe in deeply as a new question appeared.

WHAT IS THE ONLY SPECIES OF DEER TO NOT HAVE ANTLERS

My breath caught in my throat, and my stomach sank. There was the mention of deer again, the animal present in every house so far, even if it was subtle. I could feel myself blink rapidly, trying to keep my body from shifting into overdrive.

The countdown began.

10…9…8…

"Shit, I have no idea," Connor said aloud to me and Mia.

"Me either," Mia replied, her voice still shaken.

I looked down at the choices.

SCOTTISH RED DEER
CHINESE WATER DEER
MULE DEER
SIKA DEER

My heart was trying to jump out of my chest. I couldn't focus on the correct answer; all I could think about was that these deer, *these antlers,* were constantly following me, guiding me on a path that only I belonged on.

5…4…3…

"I'm guessing the red deer," Mia whispered as she chose the answer, her tone monotonous, like she couldn't give a shit if she got it right or not. Connor must've heard her, because he tapped the same square on his screen upon hearing her words.

Something inside me was screaming that the answer they picked was wrong. I couldn't place why, and I couldn't tell you a single thing about any of these deer, but there was a deep, nagging feeling that told me to pick something else. For some reason, the Chinese Water Deer stuck out to me, and I had no idea why.

2…

With only a single second to decide, I gave in to the urge to follow my gut.

1…

I tapped the second square on the screen and looked up. The countdown was gone, and our results appeared.

INCORRECT

My heart dropped at the sight of the word. Were we all incorrect? Was I the only one that was wrong? I quickly glanced to Connor, then to Mia, who had her eyes tightly squeezed shut. How were we supposed to know—

The floor on both sides of me opened, dropping Mia and Connor simultaneously. There was a sliver of a scream that came from Mia, but it was gone before I could hear it. The black square engulfed them, sucking them into the depths of the unknown, keeping them trapped.

A whimper escaped me as I was alone, all alone, trying to stay afloat. My skin was covered in goosebumps from head to toe as my hands held a death grip on the podium. How many questions do I have to answer until I can leave? Do I even *want* to leave without the others? Walking through the rest of the haunted house alone seemed like the absolute worst-case scenario.

I didn't want to be alone.

I *can't* be alone.

Not with The Man around, watching me, waiting for me.

A new question appeared on the screen as I breathed heavily.

$$(18 \div 6 \times 5) - 14 \div 7 = \underline{\qquad}$$

Fuck. *Fuck!*

10…9…8…

I immediately began to solve the equation. Parentheses. Eighteen divided by six is three. Three times five is fifteen.

5…4…3…

Fourteen divided by seven is two.

2…

Fifteen minus two is thirteen.

The answer is thirteen.

I reached for the screen, but as soon as I tried to tap the square, the answers vanished.

No, no, *no.*

Furiously, I tapped the screen where the correct answer once was, but nothing happened.

I took too long. I was too late.

With my hands still hovering over the screen in the podium, I peered up to the screen on the wall. The equation was gone, along with the timer.

I lost.

The floor below me opened, and I dropped into a pit of blackness. My stomach felt like it catapulted into my throat as gravity sucked me down, the air in my lungs squeezing away with every inch of freefall.

Lower and lower, I went.

Deeper.

Deeper.

My descent was long, or so it felt.

My mind was blank, my thoughts were gone, my fear was my entirety.

Then, I hit something soft and billowy. The material cradled me as my hands grasped for something, anything, to pull myself up and out of the surrounding hold. It took my mind a second to process what had happened and where I was, but I soon realized I had fallen onto a giant inflated mat.

My hands felt the smooth plastic. It was soft, it was clean, and it caught my fall.

Glancing up at the floor I just fell through, I could see a slight outline of the trap door, thanks to the light from the ceiling above it. The drop had to be at least thirty to forty feet down.

So maybe the fall wasn't as high as I thought, but when you're falling into the unknown, the descent feels like hours.

I looked ahead. There was nothing but a long hallway of darkness with no end in sight.

Then, there was a loud banging to my left. My head snapped to the side, only to see Connor trying to get my attention. He was separated from me by a thick sheet of clear plexiglass. I approached him slowly, studying the divider between us, reaching out to touch it. Along the wall behind him were sconces, just like the ones from the bathroom at the front of the park. They cast a luminous glow behind another sheet of plexiglass, setting a dark, ominous mood, adding to all the dread this place had to offer.

"Sadie! Are you okay?" Connor asked, his voice muffled through the glass.

I nodded, then looked to my right. Mia and Elliot were standing up, watching me. They were also separated by clear plexiglass, with both Mia and Elliot in their own sections.

It's like we were mice in a maze.

The air mats behind us began to deflate quickly with a hiss.

"What now?" Mia shouted, looking between me and Elliot. He shrugged, and I furrowed my eyebrows.

Something wasn't right.

Why were we separated yet still able to see each other? There has to be a point to this. There has to be a reason why we can't be with each other.

Suddenly, I heard a clicking sound behind me.

Tick, tick, tick.

The others heard it, too, because the four of us turned around to look at the dark, shadowed wall. I couldn't see anything, even though my eyes had already adjusted to the lack of lighting.

But that's when I noticed the others beginning to panic. Their walls were moving toward them, between their sheets of plexiglass, pushing the deflated heap of plastic on the ground with it. They were being shoved into the dark void behind them.

I looked to Connor, who was slowly backing up, and then I looked to Mia, who was doing the same. But when I looked at my wall, nothing was happening. I was standing still as the others were being pushed away. Their walls were starting to propel faster, forcing them to move quicker. I tried to follow and walk with them, even though I was the only one not being forced to.

"What's going on?" Connor asked me, a confused look in his eye. He turned to face the moving wall, putting his palms flat against it, trying to push back. His efforts were futile. The wall was stronger than him.

But before I could say anything, I felt arms wrap around me from behind, pinning my arms to my sides. I let out a yelp as I was lifted off the ground, with my feet kicking and my legs flailing.

"Sadie!" I heard both Mia and Connor scream for me. Connor pounded on the plexiglass between us, but his wall continued to push him away. The walls were moving faster now, forcing the others into a run that led them away from me.

I continued to thrash around, trying to loosen the grip that was held on me, but it was too tight. A strong scent of sandalwood surrounded me, like the smell of the crashing ocean or a serene waterfall. Without looking, without seeing him, I knew who was there. I knew who had me.

It was The Man.

I could feel his breath hot on my neck as he breathed me in, his nose brushing against my skin through his mask. In an attempt to cast him off balance, I tried to throw my shoulders back as he lifted me, but he was firmly planted on the ground. My strength was no match for him. He was too big, too strong.

And he was enjoying this too much.

I could hear the others continuing to pound on the plexiglass, but the sounds drifted away as they were pushed to the other end of the hallway.

The Man lowered me only by a few inches, and I could feel the pressure of his hard cock pressing against my ass. I could feel his breath quicken, the rise and fall of his chest against my back becoming just a hint more rapid. Taking one arm, he moved his large, gloved hand slowly down my side until it reached the top of my thigh. My eyes fluttered closed at the sensation, at the intimacy of it, and I absentmindedly rolled my hips.

His masked face was still breathing against my neck, smelling my delicate skin, smelling the pheromones emitting my fear.

With his hand still on me, I could feel the heat of him through my jeans, and I decided to use that fire to my advantage. His palm slipped to the inside of my thigh, and I knew this was my chance.

With a quick twist of my body, I slipped out of his one-armed hold. His arms fell away from me as I stumbled forward, catching myself before completely falling.

Then, I ran.

I ran as fast as I could down the black hallway without looking back. I ran to catch up to the others, who were already long gone. With my hands and arms stretched out in front of me, I cautiously prepared for some sort of ending, some type of exit.

I ran and ran and ran, with my knees shaking and my throat burning.

I ran until my body hit a door. I flung it open and stumbled out into the night, collapsing on the ground where the others were waiting for me.

Dirt slid under my palms and scuffed the knees of my jeans as I turned my body, quickly looking back to the door I just fell through. I was fully expecting The Man to have followed me and chased me out, but he didn't.

I came out alone.

2:12 AM

Not a second went by before Connor and Elliot helped me to my feet, lifting me and steadying me. I brushed the loose dirt off my clothes as they stared at me.

"What the hell?" Connor asked.

"Who the *fuck* does that guy think he is?" Elliot sneered, moving back to wrap his arm tightly around Mia. Even though she also looked unimpressed, she still checked in with me.

"Are you okay?"

"I'm fine. It's fine," I began, saying the words more to myself than them as I pretended to study my clothes for extra dirt. I refused to look at any of them after what just happened. The Man grabbed me in complete darkness, wrapped me in his arms from behind, and held me captive. For a second there, *I didn't completely hate it,* even though I knew I was supposed to. The thudding in my chest and the race in my pulse proved it. I was supposed to be angry and upset for experiencing something like that.

But I wasn't sure I could be.

Part of me liked the way his big arms squeezed me, the way his masked face brushed against my neck, and the way he effortlessly pinned my body to his.

Through all the fear and commotion, he sought me out and found me.

I snapped out of the thought and shook my head.

"It's fine," I echoed, a slight crack in my voice defying my words. Brushing the hair out of my face, I lifted my chin to look up at them. They all held a worried expression as they stared at me.

"How many times do I have to say it? It's fake." I shrugged. "It's what we signed up for."

"Sadie," Mia spoke, almost condescendingly. "There's no way you can think any of this is fake anymore. These people are *fucking* psycho. How can you defend this?"

"Defend *what*? The fact that they're actually scaring you at a haunted house?"

"That guy just grabbed you without your consent! And those other people in there grabbed me, too. That's not how a haunted house should be. They're taking advantage of people who want to have fun. It's *assault.*" Her voice grew louder with fury, and I could hear the seriousness in her words.

"Come on, Mia. They're *allowed* to do that stuff. Remember the disclaimer at the first house?"

"They said *touch*, not grab. Definitely not *grope.*" She was practically spitting her words out at me.

"Okay, okay," Connor stepped in, placing his arms between us. "How about we just go through the last house, then we can call it a night, yeah?"

A few silent moments passed before I nodded, tearing my eyes away from an angry Mia.

Elliot sighed. "I would, but..."

He pulled up his sleeve and held up his wrist, which was bare.

"...I lost my bracelet. I think one of those corpses back there accidentally pulled it off when I was trying to get to Mia."

"Good," Mia replied. "I wasn't about to go in, anyway."

I fought every urge to roll my eyes before turning to her again. Forcing empathy in my tone, I spoke. "I'm sorry, Mia, that you aren't having fun. That's the point of this, right? To be scared and have fun?"

I looked at her as she held her elbow with no reaction to my words.

"I'm sorry for pushing you into going through that last house. I shouldn't have done that. If you want to be done, we can be done."

Mia glanced at me, a softness filling the creases of her expression. She slowly nodded her head as Elliot gave her a gentle squeeze, and I dropped my shoulders.

I would never want to push someone into doing something they didn't want to do. If she wanted to go home, she could go. Of course, I wanted to go into the last house, but there was no way I was going to go through it alone.

So, I waved my white flag. If it wasn't for Mia inviting me along tonight, I wouldn't have been able to experience any of it.

We turned to leave, my steps heavy in defeat, before Connor cleared his throat.

"If you want, Sadie, I'll go through the last one with you."

I paused at his words as my footsteps stilled. Was he really willing to go through it, just the two of us? A small pang of excitement sparked in me before quickly snuffing itself out.

Once again, the image of The Man struck me, and I knew this wasn't a good idea. I hesitated, trying to choose my words carefully, but came up short.

Elliot took Connor's offer to his benefit. "Yeah, you guys go ahead. We can meet you back at the parking lot." He gave Mia a sly look, planting a kiss on the side of her head before they both eased past us.

After watching them head back to their car, I looked to Connor, who never took his eyes off me. He raised his eyebrows.

"What do you say?"

A wave of uncertainty rushed through my insides. "I don't know. I should probably get back to my friend. She's probably sleeping in her car, waiting for me."

Pulling my phone out of my pocket, I checked it for the first time since Mia invited me to join her. The screen was blank. There were no messages or missed calls, but that might have been because of the lack of cell phone service here. I tucked my phone away and sighed.

Everything in me was screaming at me to not do this. To go home. To leave the night unfinished.

But there was a gleam in Connor's eye, like a small glimmer of hope, and a little piece of me broke. He has been nothing but a gentleman to me tonight. He's been my guide every step of the way, and he was constantly checking to see if I was alright. Having him close was like a breath of fresh air, but I knew it wasn't in the cards for me.

Or for us.

Tilting my head to the side, I choked out his name. "Connor…"

He stopped me. "No, it's alright." He flashed a sympathetic yet sincere grin. "I understand."

As he slid his hands into his pockets, he began to walk, and I stepped alongside him.

After a brief moment of comfortable silence, with the moonlight shining on the side of his face, he spoke again. "Guess we'll never know what that last one is like."

His words made me stop in my tracks. Connor only took a few more steps before he stopped as well, then turned to face me. We made eye contact, and he narrowed his eyebrows, confused.

A small smirk curled up on my lips.

"Fuck it. Let's do it."

2:23 AM

THE NIGHT

Darkness guided us to the final house. When we reached the entrance, we felt completely alone. There were no other guests, no line to wait in, and nothing to remind us that this was all part of the experience. No more food trucks, no more picnic tables, no more actors lurking in the shadows. The woods were quiet, almost seeming peaceful and tranquil.

But we knew better.

Connor and I approached the tree line, where one man sat on a chair, his back against a tree. He wore black from head to toe, with the hood of his sweatshirt pulled up. Shadows ran down the entire front of him, and we were unable to see his face. He held up scissors, and Connor and I let him cut our bracelets. Once he was done, he leaned back in his chair and crossed his arms.

Assuming that meant we could go, we stepped past him and into the woods.

There was a dirt path, probably about six feet wide, that led us into the depths of the trees. Everything around us was dark and shadowed.

It would be completely black if it wasn't for the sliver of moonlight in the sky above, but even that was shielded by thick, grey clouds. But it was our only source of light, and my eyes absorbed every bit of it as possible.

There were no guides. No lasers or chain fences. No bright tape, no ropes to keep us within certain limits, nothing that would allude to us being in a haunted house.

Could you even consider this a haunted house? Maybe a haunted forest? Did we step into a twisted version of a haunted maze?

We walked side by side, with Connor leading the way by just a half-step. My arm nestled in under his, keeping close in our journey. We both remained quiet as we walked and listened for any sound that could throw us off. So far, the path was eerily quiet, and my heartbeat wasn't close to slowing down.

After finding ourselves deeper in the woods, about a half mile in, there was a snapping sound behind us. We both stopped and turned to the noise.

"Can you see anything?" Connor whispered, his face leaning close to mine.

"No," I whispered back.

With our hearing on high alert, we waited a few moments before resuming our walk. Our steps were lighter and faster now that we were hyper-aware of the potential of someone behind us.

The path led us in twists and turns, in valleys and hills, between close trees, and in forks that soon rejoined.

Another snap of a branch sounded behind us, and Connor didn't bother to turn around this time.

"We're being followed," he said briskly.

I nodded. "That's to be expected here."

Even though my voice was confident and my words were true, there was an anxious feeling brewing in the pit of my stomach.

There was a reason why we were the only ones left in the whole park. No one wanted to tough it out, and for good reason. These haunted houses weren't for the weak; they weren't for the faint of heart.

They had blood, confusion, and entrapment. We solved puzzles, our senses ran into overdrive, and we even fell from high heights.

This place was for those who enjoyed the chase.

For those who wanted to be hunted.

For those who lived joyously in the fear.

I was one of those people.

Connor placed his hand between my shoulder blades, guiding me in front of him, guarding my backside. I led the way, pushing a branch away that was hovering over the path.

There was a crack to our right, and my steps picked up speed, my feet moving in a slow jog. Connor kept my pace as another branch broke to our left, and I could hear him curse under his breath.

"Go, Sadie, go," Connor commanded behind me, his voice quiet so only I could hear.

I started to run, and I could hear Connor's steps in speed with mine. My boots thudded on the hard, cold ground, and Connor's sneakers scuffed in the dirt below.

There were level footsteps behind us that picked up pace as well, keeping a steady tempo with us. I lifted my knees higher and pushed my legs harder in my run. I ducked under branches and dodged slim trees. Connor mimicked my motions since there wasn't enough light for him to see ahead and anticipate what was to come.

Leaves rustled to our left, and I knew whoever was following us wasn't letting up. They knew these woods better than we did.

As I ran, the toe of my boot caught on a tree root that was lifted through the ground. I tripped and landed hard on my chest, my lungs expelling an *umph* up through my throat. My face hit the dirt, and my cheek scratched on the rocks and rough terrain. In the fall, I squeezed my eyes shut tight, but once I was on the ground, I opened them quickly. Right in front of me was a tree, knocked over on its side, the trunk splintered open. There were wooden daggers only inches from my face, taunting me, causing my eyes to go wide with fear. One inch to the left, and I could've split my face open.

Connor had just enough reaction time to jump over my legs, turn around, and kneel down to me.

"Are you okay?" he asked, slightly out of breath as he grabbed my arms.

Backing away from the tree, I nodded. "Yeah, I'm good."

Before my words were fully out, Connor began pulling me away from the fall and back into our run. But within our first few steps, I noticed something didn't look right. The path was clear, open, and inviting.

Too inviting.

"Wait, *wait*," I demanded, grabbing Connor's arm before he could take another step. His head turned to me, his neck pulsing with his elevated heart rate.

Silently, I motioned to the ground in front of us. Connor looked, his head tilted to the side, then kneeled down.

My heart dropped.

Only one step away was a thin, clear fishing line. It ran from one side of the path to the other. Hesitantly, he reached down to touch it, his fingertips gently running along the taught line.

As he studied it, I listened to the sounds behind me. There were more footsteps, fallen leaves crunching under each one. This time, the steps were slower and more deliberate. A chill ran through my body at the thought of someone watching me, waiting for me.

Hunting me.

Connor pulled the line in front of him, and suddenly, a heavy, black net coiled up in a tree.

It was a trap.

Still holding the fishing line, Connor looked back at me. "How did you know?"

I gave a simple shrug in response right as a loud *snap* rang through the air.

"What the—"

Snap snap snap snap snap.

More sounds cracked through the air, bursting in our direction. Without thinking, I ran, and Connor immediately followed.

Snap snap snap snap snap.

Whatever it was, it was following us, keeping the distance consistent, but the snaps were louder than their echo, and I knew it was closer than I could envision.

Then, with the whip of a *zing* flying by my ear and a springing recoil, I registered a new sound, one that was different than before.

Without stopping, I turned to look behind me. In a tree, one that was to my right as I ran by it, was an arrow sticking out of the wood.

They were actually fucking hunting us.

If the person would've shot the arrow a half second sooner, it would've pierced me right in my ear.

"Arrows," I conveyed to Connor, who I'm sure heard the noise as well.

With more arrows and more snaps, we ran until we reached a tree with low branches and lunged for it. We ducked down, our knees pressed hard on the ground as we crawled off the path and behind the tree.

Breathing heavily, I looked at Connor. "I know those were arrows, but what was that other sound?"

He looked around briefly before nodding his head over me, motioning to a spot over my shoulder. "Look," he said, and I turned.

There was a tree covered in bright red paint splatter, a handful of circles decorating the bark.

"Someone has a paintball gun," Connor whispered. I looked back at him, and his soft eyes met mine, barely visible in the hidden October moonlight.

Both of our chests were heaving from the excitement and the emotions that came to the surface. His eyes glanced down to my lips, only for a fraction of a second before another round of *snaps* filled the air.

Snap snap snap snap snap.

The tree directly to my right lit up with bright red paint. Everything in me was begging to get up and run, but instead, Connor reached over me and brushed his fingers along the bark, taking traces of paint off with his skin. He rubbed it between his fingers, his eyebrows slanting downward.

"This is runny."

I frowned, confused.

He elaborated as he pulled me away from the targeted tree. "This isn't just paint, Sadie. This is paint mixed with something else."

I looked down at his fingers. He was right. There were bright red swirls in the liquid, but it wasn't thick like regular paint. I studied it, pulling his hand closer to my face, my vision trying to cut through the darkness.

There were dark red streaks mixed in.

I knew instantly.

It was blood.

"Go," I barked to Connor, who didn't spare a second thought before grabbing my wrist and pulling me. His red fingerprints dotted my sleeve as he refused to let me go. We ran off the path and through the woods, trying our best to stay quiet, but the leaves crunching and the branches snapping deceived us. We were constantly stumbling over logs, tripping into pits of branches, and falling into nature's dips that we were unable to see.

Snap snap snap snap snap.

More paintball shots rang out, but now they sounded like they were farther away. They landed on the ground beside us, and their impact wasn't as strong. Connor and I kept our pace as we tried to find our way out. We managed to dodge the paintballs and arrows, never stopping long enough to give the shooters a steady target. I could feel the brush of wind against the backs of my legs as every arrow missed me, only skimming the denim of my jeans.

Connor's grip remained tight on me, which I was thankful for, because without it I'd be lost. I couldn't see *anything* besides the outline of his shoulders and the red paint splatter around us, and Connor's long legs had a bigger stride than I could keep up with by myself.

Snap snap snap snap snap.

"Fuck," Connor bit out, and I knew he was hit, but he didn't even pause to look. My eyes scanned his body before landing on his leg. There was red paint on the outside of his right knee.

"At least it wasn't an arrow," he said calmly as he kept his pace, and I was impressed at his ability to press on.

We continued to trot through the dense woods, squeezing our way through untouched trees, high bushes, and constant foliage. There was mud at our feet and scratches on our skin. There were crickets chirping and owls hooting.

But we kept going.

And going.

And going.

Snap snap snap snap snap.

Now, these paintball shots were close.

Too close.

I felt a sudden sharp pain on my right hip. I let out a yelp, and there was no hesitation as Connor whipped around to face me.

"*Fuck*, Sadie, that wasn't an arrow, right? Are you okay? Let me see."

Ignoring him, I pushed past where he stood and hurried on. I didn't want to stand here and risk getting hit again. He followed, a heavy exhale escaping past his lips in acceptance that I wasn't going to pause this chase just yet.

My path led us through the forest as a slender twig with leaves got stuck in my hair. I quickly yanked it out and threw it to the side. Our steps were quick until they brought us to a hollow, black opening. It was hidden in the side of a hill, not too tall but big enough to notice. Heavy branches and dark moss covered the arch, shadowing its identity, but there was no doubt about what it was.

My eyes widened.

"Is this—" Connor began.

I finished his question. "The Alkene Caves."

From what I could see after quickly glancing around, there was only one. There may be more, but in this darkness, I couldn't tell.

I moved closer to the entrance, my steps slow and reluctant. I wasn't sure if there was something—or someone—waiting for us in there, but the itching, burning need to find out was more than I could bear.

Pulling my phone out of my pocket, I turned the flashlight on and brought it to eye level. When I pointed it to the entrance, the light didn't do much to penetrate the darkness. All I could see were dark, dirt-coated walls, and an abyss into nothing.

There was no sound, there was no movement, there was no sign of life.

I swallowed my reluctance, my breathing suspended as I took one final step closer.

Standing on the edge of the cave, Connor reached out and touched my arm. "Sadie, are you hurt?"

At the mention of it, my mind was brought back to the pain flaring in my skin. We looked down at my sweatshirt with my flashlight, looking at the bright red splotch on my side. Connor tried to lift the hem to get a better look, but I pushed his hands away.

"I'm fine," I said defensively, even though my side was throbbing. "Forget this. We need to keep going."

"Sadie—"

"Please, *let's go.*"

My voice was aching with need, and my plea was deeply rooted in my soul. He blinked, acknowledging me, and then turned to keep going.

We left the mysterious cave and ran through another long stretch of woods, and the paintball shots seemed to have stopped. Now, there were no more footsteps, no more trip lines, and no more snaps. With our lungs burning and our legs exhausted, our journey began to slow down. I didn't even know if we were heading in the right direction.

Connor paused, pressed his palms to his knees, and tried to catch his breath. With my hands on my hips, I tilted my head back, trying to breathe in more cold, fresh air.

"We should keep going," I suggested.

Connor looked up at me. "You sure you're okay?"

"Yeah. Are you?"

He nodded. "Yeah, I'm good."

Before we could get too comfortable in our pause, we continued walking at a leisurely pace. Our steps took us through a small, hidden path leading to a large, circular tree. With the base at least ten feet wide, the tree stood out visually from the others. We both looked at it, studying its dimensions, when there was a rustling noise coming from up in the branches.

Then, something fell.

Time seemed to stand still as everything in my body froze.

It was a human body hanging by its neck in a noose.

"Oh, my God," I shrieked, immediately falling backward onto my ass. I shuffled away from the tree, away from the sight, away from the horror, but I couldn't tear my eyes away. It was a man with dark hair and pale skin, his eyes open and empty and hollow. His mouth hung open like he was trying to scream with no voice. The rope squeezed his throat, leaving an outline of a red burn on the skin. He was dressed in a dark blue suit with a navy blue tie. His body gently swayed back and forth as his dress shoes pointed down to the ground.

He looked like an ordinary man, and that was even scarier.

Slipping behind me, Connor hooked his wrists under my arms and thrust me back onto my feet. I cried out in fear, my body suddenly feeling as if it weighed a thousand pounds. My feet struggled to carry me away, my knees buckled with each step, and my chest felt like it was chained to the same tree the man hung himself from.

A single tear rolled down my cheek as Connor repetitively whispered in my ear. "It's not real."

He had to practically carry me away from the scene as his arms held me up, his words never stopping.

"It's not real."

Over and over, he whispered it, trying to calm me down.

"It's not real."

Throughout the night, I was the one saying it to the others. I was the one who had to reiterate the fact that this was all fake. But now, alone in the woods in the middle of the night, I was the one that needed to be reminded.

I listened to Connor's quiet, soothing voice as I slowly regained my strength, and soon, I was able to force myself to walk.

"It's not real."

"It's not real."

We walked, and walked, and walked.

We walked until there was a white shimmer just beyond a set of trees.

My mind tried to tell me it was the moon, but it couldn't be. The moon was partially hidden behind dark clouds. As we got closer, we realized what it was.

It was a light.

It was a *streetlight.*

Connor and I broke out into a run, heading toward the light.

We reached the edge of the tree line, then broke free of the woods.

The streetlight shined down on a large slab of pavement where one single car resided. Its engine was on and running as exhaust fumes clouded their way up into the sky.

Leaning against that car was one person. A man with dark hair, smoking a cigarette, the smoke rising up like a wispy vapor. When he heard us stumble out of the woods, he turned to look at us, a smile rising upon his face.

"Hey, you guys made it."

It was Elliot.

We were out.

We did it.

PART TWO

Intuition tells me this is your home.
The way your breath snakes into my lungs, your oxygen is in my
blood.
My need for you is inescapable.
You may have survived, but there is more than what's at face
value.

3:37 AM

"'Bout time," Elliot began, his cigarette pinched between his fingers in one hand while he pulled his cell phone out of his pocket with the other. He tapped the screen to check the time.

"It's after three," he began with a chuckle. "What a crazy fuckin' night, right?"

Connor and I breathed heavily as we walked toward the car, neither one of us able to find any words to say. We were both shaken, our steps light and our hands trembling, but we tried not to let it show.

We were in *The Night*, then we weren't.

Whether we actually finished it or simply found the edge of the park, I wasn't sure. There may have been more to the last house than what we experienced, but what we went through was enough for me. And I'm sure Connor felt the same.

Elliot tapped the car door frame behind him, and the passenger door window rolled down. Mia poked her head out and squinted at us. She must've been sleeping, or close to it, because she was struggling to keep her eyes open.

"Hey, how was it?" she asked, her voice hoarse with sleep as we finally reached the back of the small, silver car. I could feel the slight wave of heat coming from the inside.

Connor brushed the back of his neck with his fingers, gently scratching the skin. I cleared my throat, preparing myself to act calm, but Elliot stepped in.

"Woah," he said, his eyes wide. "Is that paint?" he asked, pointing to Connor's leg.

"Yeah," Connor croaked out as he kept his eyes on his pant leg. "Paintball."

Mia looked at my right side and then the giant circle of red paint on my sweatshirt. "Sadie, you got hit too?"

I twisted my torso and looked down. "I guess so."

I wanted—no, *needed*—to see the damage done. I wanted to see it when we were at the cave, but a bigger part of me just wanted to get out of there. Grabbing the hem of my sweatshirt, I slowly lifted the side, exposing the skin underneath. Right above my hip bone was a large, purple circle, with a dark yellow welt right in the middle, like a gruesome bullseye. There were reactive goosebumps lining the circle, creating a dotted halo. Thankfully, I wasn't bleeding, but I was definitely close to it.

"Damn, Sadie." Elliot exhaled.

Connor looked from my welt to my eyes, a sliver of hurt shining through his expression, almost as if he was disappointed that he couldn't shield me or protect me. After a sober moment, Connor dropped his gaze away from me.

"Oh my God, are you alright?" Mia asked through the window. I nodded through my continued stare toward Connor, my vision watching the way he shifted uncomfortably. I lowered my sweatshirt, careful not to drag the fabric over the wounded skin.

"What about your leg, Connor?" Mia asked. "Does it hurt?"

Connor shook his head. "Nah, it's not bad. They were pretty far away when they got me."

Mia nodded, and Elliot took another drag of his cigarette. "So, what was it like in there?" he asked, exhaling the smoke.

"It was…" Connor began, but his voice trailed off, so I finished his sentence for him.

"Exhilarating."

Once again, Connor looked at me with eyes made of stone, but I wasn't lying. I met his stare in a conversation that wasn't viable with spoken words. I could tell he was trying to figure out if I was bluffing or not, but the only way he could really find out if I was telling the truth was if he reached down the front of my jeans to feel the wetness in my underwear.

Both Mia and Elliot flashed an easy grin, and I could tell they weren't really interested in hearing about the final house. Then again, they were never that enthusiastic about this place from the beginning.

I did a quick scan of the empty parking lot and let out a deep sigh. "Well, since there's no bright blue Jeep around, it looks like Miranda went home without me."

"What a good friend," Mia said sarcastically, her arm resting on the window frame.

I ignored her, pulled my cell phone out of my pocket, and unlocked it. I still had no service, which meant I was unable to receive any text messages or calls.

"Want a ride?" Elliot asked.

I shook my head. "Oh, that's okay. I can get an Uber."

Immediately, Connor spoke up. "Hell no. We're not leaving you here."

Mia tucked herself back into the car and began to roll up the window. "He's right. Get in. It's freezing outside."

Elliot flicked the butt of his cigarette onto the pavement and got into the driver's seat.

Connor opened the back passenger door and motioned for me to get in first. I hesitated, a flash of unease spiking through me. Even though I had only met these three a few hours ago, I felt a sense of trust with them, and I knew they weren't the type to simply leave me here alone. But lingering in me, down at the bottom of my stomach, was a small but noticeable sense of foreboding.

The night had a stillness to it, as if we were the only ones up and awake in the world. My chest constricted as a chill ran down my spine.

I knew the liminal feeling would be fleeting.

My gaze met Connor's, his eyes tired and haunting, before I noticed subtle movement over his shoulder. He continued to stand at the car door as a black figure rustled in the woods behind him, filtering its way through the dark foliage.

Not a single bone in my body had to guess. I knew.

It was Him.

I didn't let any change in expression show on my face as I crawled into the car, my adrenaline not letting up even though the haunted houses were done.

The night wasn't over.

Connor sat down next to me and shut the door.

Elliot pulled out of the parking lot, his car the final one to leave, and drove out onto the road. The highway was about a half an hour out of the way, so it was easier to take the winding, hidden back roads. There were no streetlights, no painted lines in the dirt, and no other cars around. It was just us and the empty fields and forests surrounding us.

After about ten minutes of silence, I leaned forward. I could see Mia sleeping in the passenger seat, so I lowered my voice to a whisper as I spoke to Elliot.

"There's a Walmart about halfway to Petersburg if you want to drop me off there. I'll have service by then, and I can get a ride."

He nodded. "I need to stop for gas anyway."

I leaned back in my seat, letting my head hit the padding behind me. I could feel my eyelids grow heavier with every blink. There was nothing to see, nothing to watch out the window as we drove.

Only October darkness and the blanketed moon above.

We hit a bump, and Connor's knee tapped against mine. I rolled my head in his direction, only to see him already looking at me, his head resting against the seat just like mine. We stared at each other for a minute, both of us unblinking. The car was quiet as a hint of a smirk formed on his lips.

The moment was cut short as a sudden, loud burst of an engine roared behind us. Connor and I both turned to look out the rear window, and Elliot glanced in his rear-view mirror.

Through the darkness, we couldn't see much, except for the single headlight beaming through the window. The light came closer, and the sound of the engine ripped louder. It was someone on a sport bike driving behind us.

"What the fuck?" Elliot muttered, squinting his eyes away from the light reflecting in his mirror.

I swallowed the lump in my throat, my nerves suddenly creeping up my chest. This was a back road in the middle of the night. There hasn't been anyone around this whole time, except for now.

The truth in the realization was obvious.

The engine of the sport bike sparked and cracked as it continued to trail us, not bothering to keep much of a distance.

Connor looked from me to Elliot. "How much longer until we hit the gas station?"

"Only a few more miles," he replied, clearly aggravated. "Should I break-check him?"

"No," I blurted out sternly, the word coming out harsher than I intended. I knew that messing with him would only make things worse.

After all, I had no doubt in what he desired, and I feared the outcome for anyone who would get in the way.

We rode in silence as the sport bike followed us the entire way, the single headlight illuminating the inside of the car entirely. After about ten minutes, Elliot veered off into an empty parking lot of a 7/11 and pulled up next to a vacant gas pump. The sport bike revved its engine as it kept driving, speeding down the road and off into the night. Our eyes followed it as it zoomed past a few fast-food restaurants and the Walmart I mentioned earlier, and we all collectively exhaled as it disappeared.

"Fucking asshole," Elliot snarled. He opened his door, stepped out, and slammed it shut. Mia remained asleep in the passenger seat, with her neck resting on a balled-up sweatshirt and her forehead pressed against the window, oblivious to everything.

A metal clang of the gas pump sounded as the handle was inserted into the tank. Elliot leaned his back against the car and watched the numbers rise.

I looked out the front windshield to the gas station ahead. The building was cradled by more dark forest, and the lights from the inside did nothing to illuminate the woods around it.

Silence from the car's interior rang loudly in my ears, and I could feel a shift in the air. Connor moved to face me.

"Sadie…" he began, his voice soft yet hoarse, calm but aching.

A piece of my heart broke. I knew what he wanted, and what he wanted was something I couldn't give him.

"I have to go to the bathroom," I quickly blurted out as I opened my door, not leaving any room for conversation. I crossed my arms as I walked out and passed Elliot, who watched me as I went.

Connor kicked his door open and began to follow me, but I could hear Elliot stop him.

"Hey, could you grab me a Red Bull?"

Connor gave him a quick nod before heading into the store behind me. I approached the checkout counter, grabbing the attention of the clerk.

"Where's your restroom?" I asked.

The employee was an older man, probably in his late fifties, with greying hair and a grey beard to match. His eyes had deep circles, and it looked like he was sleeping right before we walked in.

"It's out on the side of the buildin'. We had a key for it, but someone broke it in the lock, so just give it a good jiggle, and it'll open right up for ya."

"Thanks." I flashed him a quick smile and turned to leave before Connor shouted to me.

"Sadie," he began, and I stopped, my hand on the door. I held my breath as I turned to look at him, unsure if I was ready to see the hurt I expected in his gaze.

"Do you want anything?" He held up two cans of Red Bull in one hand and a bag of Chex Mix in the other. The genuine smile he had the entire night was gone. "My treat."

I gently shook my head and pushed the door open.

The cool air hit me again, and goosebumps rose on my skin as I walked around the building. Sure enough, there was a door along the side, the entrance barely visible in the night. I reached out to grab the silver handle when suddenly, a hand slapped over my mouth and an arm wrapped tightly around my torso.

4:02 AM

Outside of the building, I thrashed my legs, relentlessly kicking the cement wall in front of me. My eyes began to water as my cries were silenced, my voice muffled against the large, gloved hand over my mouth. The grip was tight around my body, the arm was easily the size of one of my legs, and the pressure had my back flush against a rock-hard chest. The familiar scent of sandalwood wrapped around me, filling my lungs, and I instinctively breathed it in.

It was The Man.

It was the same scent from the person who grabbed me in *The Cloud,* almost in this same exact position. Except this time, I wasn't allowed to scream.

There was no escaping him, but I'd be damned if I didn't try.

I knew it was only a matter of minutes, maybe even seconds, before the others would come looking for me.

Trying to use the wall of the gas station to my advantage, I planted both feet flat on the cement, tilted my shoulders back, and pushed off as hard as I could. The Man stumbled back, but only by a few steps, before righting himself with me. I tried to twist and turn, my cries still buried in the palm of his hand, but nothing worked. I was simply prey caught in the teeth of its predator.

The Man dragged me into the wooded area surrounding the gas station, so I was entirely out of sight. From where we were, I could see Elliot's car. He was sitting inside, scrolling on his phone, the bright screen lighting up his face. Mia was still asleep next to him.

I began to claw at The Man's arms, trying to scratch my way free, but nothing fazed him. As I ripped against the heavy fabric of his sweatshirt, my nails briefly tore away from their beds, the skin burning at the detachment. I let out a quiet whimper, and he squeezed me tighter. His breathing was steady and controlled, while mine was rapid and erratic.

Then, I saw Connor walk out of the gas station with a bag of food and drinks. He jogged over to Elliot's car and opened the door. There was a quick look of confusion that flashed over his face as he looked around the lot. The Man was keeping me in earshot of the others so that I knew exactly what they were saying and doing, all while feeling completely helpless.

"Sadie's not back yet?" Connor's voice was quiet from the distance.

I squeezed my eyes shut as I heard Elliot speak. "No."

Then, I heard the car door shut and footsteps heading our way. I opened my eyes to see Connor at the bathroom door, gently knocking with his knuckles.

"Sadie, are you in there?" he asked, his voice hushed.

I wanted to cry, I wanted to scream, I wanted him to hear me through the gloved hand, but there was a new pressure to the underside of my jaw.

I glanced down to see a metal barrel tucked under my head, pointing up at my skull.

It was a gun.

The gloved hand that covered my mouth moved so that only The Man's index finger was resting vertically on my lips.

He was telling me to be quiet. He was shushing me.

"Sadie, are you okay?" Connor asked again as my insides trembled with terror. If he were to look behind him and walk about ten steps into the tree line, he would see me here with a gun to my jaw.

I knew that if I made a single noise, stepped on one crunchy leaf, or let out a hint of a cry, it would be game over.

My chest heaved as I remained quiet and still, my eyes wide with shock. I was *not* expecting this. Out of everything that happened tonight, out of all the scares and the games and the haunts, *this*, by far, had my blood pumping the fastest. I could feel it in my fingertips and my toes, in my chest and in my throat.

My entire being felt like it was being shocked, like I was struck by lightning twice, like I was swimming in a nightmare that had no end.

The Man palmed my mouth again, and I made no moves to stop anything from happening. I watched as Connor slowly opened the bathroom door, only to find it dark and empty. He quickly glanced around before shutting the door, then walked back to the car. He opened Elliot's door, and I could hear his voice carry over the parking lot.

"You haven't seen her?"

Elliot shook his head. "No. She's not over there?"

"No." Connor ran his hands through his hair, a wavy lock falling over his forehead as he looked distraught.

The Man removed his gloved hand from my mouth. He trailed the barrel of the gun along my jawline and up my chin, letting the tip of the metal brush against my bottom lip. His breath was warm on my neck as the metal dragged my lip down, revealing my bottom teeth.

I closed my eyes and squeezed out a tear, letting him do whatever he wanted to me.

After a few seconds of silence, Elliot asked, "Did you get her number?"

The Man's body stiffened behind me at the question, the gun still paused on my lip. I sensed Connor's hesitation from across the lot as his answer lingered on his lips.

"No."

The defeat was heavy in his voice.

The barrel of the gun moved and pushed past my lips, entering the inside of my mouth. I knew what he wanted from me, and I was in no position to deny it. With my eyes still closed, my tongue moved to meet the metal. I licked the bore of the gun, the steel cold against my wet, warm flesh. The Man reactively pressed his hips against me, satisfied with my cooperation, his strong and hard cock fitting between us.

"Well, she *did* say she was going to head up to Walmart. She's probably looking for cell service. Wanna go check?" Elliot asked.

The Man slowly moved the gun down, letting it descend down my throat, leaving a light trail of spit along the way. Over my sweatshirt, he lowered it down to my left breast, and the tip of the barrel made smooth circles around my nipple, causing it to harden.

"What? No. We can't just leave."

I heard the quick pop of the energy drink that Elliot had opened, causing me to briefly tense. "But you said she wasn't over there."

"She's not..." Connor's voice trailed off. "I don't know. Something doesn't feel right about this."

With his free hand, The Man grabbed my other breast, his thumb running over the pebbled nipple through the fabric. Memories that weren't even two hours old came back to me, when he grabbed me and ran his hands over my waist and down the inside of my thigh in *The Cloud.* I may have run from him in the end, but there was that moment of surrender that I couldn't discredit.

That same act of submission was happening now.

I tilted my head back and bit my lower lip, letting The Man caress me in a desire I've never known.

Fuck me. I was in deep.

Elliot continued. "And she's not inside the store, right?"

Connor ignored him and began to walk around the lot. "Sadie?" He shouted, calling out to me. "*Say-dee?*"

The Man slowly slid the gun down the length of my stomach, letting it fall past the button of my jeans and angling it in between my legs. He pushed the barrel firmly up against the seam, pressing on my clit through the denim. I inhaled. The pulse of my cry sat in the bottom of my ribs, echoing inside me with no escape.

"Sadie!" Connor yelled out again, his voice turning desperate. He pulled his phone out of his pocket and clicked on the flashlight, shining it in every direction possible. After checking the bathroom once again, he walked along the tree line and flashed the light into the woods. It wasn't strong enough to penetrate through the depths of the forest.

I held my breath as he walked right by me, the white of the light not coming close to touching me.

The Man pushed the gun harder against my swollen clit, slowly rubbing it in circles, a silent groan rattling my throat.

Connor took a minute to walk the perimeter of the building. After finding nothing, no footsteps or clues, he headed back to the car. He briefly took another look around, his eyes pausing on the wooded area I was in. It was like he was looking right at me but not seeing me at all.

He knew something wasn't right. Something was off.

"Okay," he finally spoke as he opened the back car door and climbed inside. "Let's go."

"I'm telling you, she probably started walking," Elliot said before getting in behind the wheel and shutting his door.

The rest of their conversation, if there was one, was kept inside the car. I watched as they pulled out of the gas station and onto the road, heading in the direction of Walmart, the red taillights glowing in the empty field of darkness. I let out a whimper.

They left me.

I was on my own.

The Man tucked his gun away against his back in the waistband of his jeans. His hand covered my mouth once again, and his other arm slinked around the front of my torso. With my body pushed in front of him, he began to walk forward, keeping me close to him and squeezing me with every step. It was his way of letting me know there was no chance of me slipping away. I walked with him, letting him guide me to where he wanted to take me.

I needed to keep myself strong and find an easy way to fight. Now was not the time to try and run. If I could even get away, where would I go? Would I run after Elliot's car and try to flag them down? There's no way The Man would let me get that far.

I needed to think; I needed to be focused. I needed to cooperate.

He led me through the woods to a side road, one that was completely dark and away from the lights of the other buildings. On the edge of the tree line was his silver sport bike, the one I saw him on as he followed us.

Either he turned around after speeding off, or he never completely drove away.

My knees began to lock up as he pushed me closer to the bike, my cries still locked under his hand. He wanted to take me somewhere. But where?

I glanced to the back of the bike, where two helmets hung off the edge.

Two.

He had this planned.

He glanced at me before releasing his hand from my mouth, unsure if he could trust me. I kept it closed.

Even if I screamed now, there was no one around to hear me.

As if reading my thoughts and sensing my fear, The Man grabbed me and spun me around to face him. He was still covered from head to toe in black, with black jeans, a black sweatshirt, black gloves, and a black mask. The only thing I could see were his eyes, the same eyes that followed me multiple times throughout the night. They flickered back and forth between mine, his irises thin in the darkness. He watched me, studying me for any fear I might have, any fight I was willing to give.

I should fight. I should run.

In a split-second decision, I tore myself away from the situation and began to run. My boots scuffed on the dirt road as I took off, but I only made it a few feet before The Man's arms were back around my waist. I fell forward from the momentum, my fingers barely brushing the cold dirt road as The Man held me tight.

Deep in my chest sat all the screams I wanted to project, but the only thing I could force out was a low, heavy cry. The Man picked me up effortlessly and carried me back to the sport bike in only a few steps.

He was stronger and faster. I had no chance.

When he placed me back on my feet, all I did was stare at him with a tearful apprehension in my eyes and unrest in my bones.

Grabbing a helmet, he shoved it over my head, pushing it down tight as my hair cascaded down my shoulders. It fit snugly against my skull.

Then, with a quick snap of his arm, he whipped out a white rope from his sweatshirt pocket. He reached down, grabbed one of my arms, and began to wrap the rope around my wrist. It was tight, almost too tight, as he wound it around my skin. He pulled on the rope, making sure it couldn't unravel, and dragged me toward the seat like a dog on a leash.

My heart began to beat faster.

He grabbed me by my hips and lifted me, placing me onto the back of the bike. Still holding onto the rope, he swung his leg over his seat, planting himself in front of me.

Then, he reached back to grab my other arm, but I moved it away. "No."

His head snapped to look at me, anger lighting up the only part of him I could see.

Without second guessing anything, I twisted my body, trying to shimmy off the bike, but his arms reached around and grabbed me before I could find a way down. My wrist was still bound by the rope, and through the struggle, it was beginning to burn me.

"Let me go," I commanded quietly, but he ignored me.

With my body still sitting on the back of the bike, he reached for my other arm again, but I repeated the same motion. I pulled it up to my chest, not letting him have it. My dignity didn't want to let him win.

"I don't want to."

My voice began to quiver, deceiving me. There was a drive of adrenaline still pumping through me, and a piece of me wasn't fighting this, even though I knew I was supposed to. I wasn't supposed to let a big man in a dark mask tie me up and take me away.

But then, there was the thought of him watching me as I waited in line with Mia.

Watching me walk through *The Eternity* as he sat at the dining room table.

Capturing me in his arms, pinning me to him, after falling in *The Cloud.*

There was the thought of his breath on my neck.

His hand over my breast.

My ass pressing into his stiff cock.

He blinked at me, and he knew I wanted this.

Did I want this?

For the third time, he reached back and grabbed my arm. This try, he got it and pulled me forward, forcing my hands to meet in front of him. He tied my wrists, the bones rubbing together, the rope securing me in my position.

My face was less than an inch away from his back as the rest of my body cradled into him. Nestled right against my slick center, I could feel his gun in the waistband of his jeans, and if I moved just right, the shape of it pressed against me in the most satisfying places.

But instead, I focused on the same sandalwood scent from earlier wafting off of him. I couldn't help but take in a deep breath, letting the rich aroma fill my lungs and work my nerves just as much as the gun.

Once he was done with the rope, he grabbed his helmet and pushed it on, only adding to the mystery of him. I looked at the back of it and noticed a little decal on the bottom.

It was a black silhouette of a deer head.

I swallowed hard.

The deer. They were *everywhere.*

The Man turned on the bike and revved the engine. Leaning forward, the wheels rolled, and he began to drive. With the force of the start, my body leaned back as my bound wrists pressed into his chest, where I then instinctively held onto him. At first, we went slow, but after a minute, he began to pick up speed.

It was the middle of the night, and we were on the back roads. There was absolutely no one around.

No one to question why we were out, where we were going, or why I was tied up.

Feeling the steadiness of the bike, I let my body feel the turns, leaning into the tilt and balance. I trusted the ride, I trusted the drive, and I trusted The Man who knew how to operate it all.

Although my heartbeat never slowed down.

His big, gloved hands gripped the handles, effortlessly switching between the throttle and brake when needed. Just from the beginning of this ride alone, I could tell riding this bike was like second nature to him, and I'd be lying if I said it wasn't attractive as hell.

My gaze roamed up his covered arms to his shoulders, and even through the sweatshirt, I could see his strong muscles tensing and releasing, working to keep the ride smooth.

I glanced up to his helmet, peering around the side to get a better view of the mystery. He kept his face forward as he watched the dark roads in front of him. Even though he still had his mask on under the helmet, I couldn't help but wonder what he looked like at that moment. I wondered if his skin was glistening with sweat or if he could see me out of his peripheral vision.

The thought vanished as we took a hard turn, forcing me to lean with him to accommodate.

After a few miles, I noticed my hands were beginning to hurt. Between the cold October air and the speed of the bike, the exposure felt like thousands of needles poking every inch of my skin. I tried rubbing my hands together, but the ropes and the placement of my wrists made it impossible. Another mile rolled by, and I was starting to tear up from the pain. I cried out, the sound hindered by the helmet and the roar of the engine. I didn't need to see my hands to know they were beginning to turn a shade of blue.

I was desperate for warmth, for relief.

Slowly and gently, I lowered my hands down, letting them rest on the lap of The Man. He didn't seem to notice, and if he did, he didn't care. He was too focused on the drive.

I squeezed my eyes shut, then moved to grab the hem of his sweatshirt. Suddenly, his back muscles tensed. He knew what I was doing.

I buried my hands underneath his sweatshirt, feeling immediate relief.

Oh my *God*, the *warmth*.

I could easily bury my whole body underneath this sweatshirt just to feel warm.

My hands brushed against the smooth skin of his stomach, his firm muscles tightening under my touch.

I wasn't sure if he was too occupied by driving to pull my hands away or if he didn't mind having them there. And I wasn't sure why I cared. I was *fucking tied up*.

Through the helmet, I watched the back of The Man as he concentrated on the road. All I could see was a small sliver of inked skin between his mask and the hood of his sweatshirt, peeking out from under his helmet.

I stared at that line of skin for the rest of the way.

Before I knew it, the bike slowed down to a stop, with The Man's feet planted on the ground to balance us. I looked around, trying to figure out where we were.

And that's when I saw the gates.

We were back at *Inferno's Edge*.

The Man slipped off his helmet, careful not to take the mask off with it. Then, he reached down and untied my wrists, revealing red and inflamed skin. They hurt, but at least they weren't as cold anymore. Once the rope was gone, I moved my arms away from him, bringing them back into my chest. We both got off the bike, with him swinging his leg over as I slid off the back of the bike. I pulled the helmet off and tossed it forcefully to him, giving him only a split second of reaction time to catch it, but he did. I stood there, fearfully still, watching him as he calmly set both helmets on the back of the bike.

There was a sense of doom brewing in the pit of my stomach. To me, time always felt different in the middle of the night. The world was asleep, unaware of the evil that awoke in the darkness. There was an unexplainable feeling, one that I always got if I was awake this late. It ran through every cell in my body, warning me of what was to come.

I could feel it now, stronger than ever, standing here.

Staring at The Man as he stared back at me.

It was like the haunted houses were even more haunted now that no one was around.

I pushed the thoughts away and shivered.

"What do you want?" I whispered, barely audible.

He looked at me, unwilling to give me an answer before walking toward the front gates.

The gate I was just at, only hours ago, with Mia, Connor, and Elliot.

The gate that began the night and is now the beginning of the end.

In the middle of the entrance was a post, and on the post was a silver keypad. The Man entered a code, which in turn caused a buzzing sound, then a click. He pushed the gates open wide, then turned back to me.

My eyes stayed on his the whole time as he approached me, his height towering over me.

Then, he drifted behind me, and before I knew it, his arms were back around me, pinning me to him.

But this time, he didn't cover my mouth. There was no reason to. There was no one around.

Inferno's Edge was on acres upon acres of land with no civilization for miles.

The haunted houses had a different feel to them now as opposed to earlier. When they were open, they were meant to be scary. Now, with their gates closed and their doors shut, they were scary without trying to be.

All of the employees, the actors, the volunteers, they were all gone.
All of them.
We were alone.
Just me and The Man.
Alone.
And I screamed.

4:27 AM

Yelling did nothing to help, but I did it anyway. I screamed, I thrashed, I cried, I grunted, all while trying to tear myself away from The Man. But his arms were locked around me like an iron chain, his strength unbreakable as he caught my every move.

"Fuck!" I screamed. "Fucking let me go!"

His only response was a squeeze of his arms as he walked.

We made our way along the front path, and I knew exactly where he was taking me.

In between my steps, I would buck against him and kick the air, and he would end up lifting and carrying me in large strides. He wasn't putting up with any of my shit, no matter how much of it I was giving him.

We came upon the first haunted house, *The Asylum,* and he kicked in the door. It swung wide open, slamming against the wall behind it. We entered, and the door slowly fell closed behind us. I continued to scream, but now my voice was trapped inside the walls where screams were normalized.

The Man made his way through the black maze easily, even with no lights on. With me against his front, trying to fight him away, he knew every turn and every corner without needing lasers to guide him.

Things looked the same, yet different. In the first room, there was the same chair as earlier, but without anyone sitting in it. I looked up to see the deer's head still hung up on the wall. Instead of going straight through, The Man took me off to the side and pushed open a hidden wall. I didn't even notice it when I was here earlier, probably because everything was so dim, and the shadows were heavy. He dragged me through the wall, and we found ourselves in the area that was meant to resemble a hospital. We skipped the bloody bathroom, the rubber suffocation tunnel, and the rest of the black hallways.

It was a shortcut.

As we passed the viewing window, my mind flickered back to earlier in the night when Connor flipped the switch and electrocuted the patient on the bed.

Except now, there were no doctors, there was no patient, and there was no need to turn the machines on.

Or so I'd hoped.

The bright, blinding lights were still on as The Man pushed me into the room and threw me onto the bed. I rolled but caught myself before I could fall off. My hands gripped the mattress, my knuckles snow white, as my body immediately sat up straight.

"Please," I begged. "Don't."

The Man flicked on the machines, and they all lit up, a whirring sound filling the room. When I looked around, I noticed another deer head mounted above the viewing window. I didn't see it earlier in the night, but then again, I didn't actually come into the room until now. My eyes locked on the animal as its hollow eyes stared at the wall across from it. I swallowed the lump in my throat and broke my stare, moving my gaze down to the bed. Blue and red cords were hanging from the side, and The Man grabbed them the second he saw me eye them.

"No—"

It was all I could manage to say before The Man pushed me back down on the bed and climbed over me. I tried to kick him off, but he sat on my hips, pinning me to the bed. I tried to wrestle with him and wiggle my way out, but he was too strong.

He moved one arm across my chest, and that was just enough to keep my upper half down. With his other hand, he pressed the sticky electrodes to my temples. I reached up to tear them away, but his arm was like a barricade, keeping me in place. Once the electrodes were attached, he reached down, pulled my sleeve up, grabbed my wrist, and forced it into the thick belt restraint. His movements were effortless as he slid the metal into the notch, securing my arm down.

With my other hand, I tried punching him in the back repeatedly, but he didn't seem to notice. It was as if I was just an annoyance to him, like a fly buzzing around his head, and my efforts to hurt him were pointless.

He turned and grabbed the wrist of that arm, mirroring the same movements as before. He pushed me down and locked me into the belt restraint.

Now I was *really* fucked.

Then, with a quick swipe over me, The Man reached over and grabbed a new mouthguard.

"No, *no*, no," I cried. I kicked my legs as hard as I could, making the metal frame of the bed rattle under my force. "Please, *please*."

Biting the plastic through his black mask, he ripped it open and pulled it out. He held it up to his face for a beat, letting me get a good look at it. He expected me to say something, to fight with my words, but when I didn't, he shoved it in my mouth. I tried to scream, but it came out as a deep-throated groan. I arched my chest as my cries vibrated the rubber in my mouth, tears from both eyes sliding down my temples.

This was supposed to be fake, *right?*

Then why did I feel the electrodes buzzing against my skin? Why could I feel a small surge against my temples?

Why did the props actually work?

With a swing of his leg, The Man climbed off of me and took a step back. His eyes never left mine as he moved to the bottom of the bed near my feet. I watched him the entire way, my breathing heavy through my nose.

I tried everything I could to wiggle myself out of the restraints. I twisted, pulled, and yanked, but nothing worked. I tried to spit the mouthguard out, but it was in too deep. My tongue failed to push it past my lips.

With his long arms, The Man reached up and grabbed the waistband of my jeans. He popped the button and unzipped the black denim, all while never tearing his gaze away from me.

I didn't think I could breathe any faster, but I did.

I didn't think my heart could pulse any harder, but it did.

His fingertips gripped the hem of my jeans, hooking them beneath my underwear and against my skin. I shook my head furiously.

Then, he pulled all of the material down, leaving me completely exposed on the bed before him. I kicked my legs, trying to shove my boots against him and his covered body, but he avoided every move I made.

I tried to push my legs together, bringing my knees up, but he grabbed them and forced them back down. The electrodes continued to buzz against my temples, the white circles tickling the skin relentlessly.

I closed my eyes with my legs down and The Man between them. Whatever he wanted, he was going to get. Even if that meant taking it without permission.

The Man rested his gloved hands on my legs, his outstretched fingers spanning the width of my thighs. They were warm and strong, and for a millisecond, I welcomed it.

He slid his palms up my bare legs, his caress subtle but noticeable. I sucked in a breath as best I could through the mouthguard. He slowly pulled his torso up onto the table, trying to get closer to me, and I let him. He moved his face into the space between my legs and inhaled. I squeezed my eyes shut.

It was invasive and it was intrusive. I was exposed and vulnerable.

I tried to blank out my mind but couldn't.

I heard fabric rustling by my legs, and I looked down to see The Man slipping off the glove of his right hand. I peered down at him and glanced at his bare hand. It was covered in ink, with letters along the fingers and a design on the back, but he was moving around too much for me to see it clearly. Through my watered eyes, the black ink just looked like a blur.

Then, without a sound, he slid his index and middle fingers along my entrance. I shuddered against the restraints. Judging by the slight growl from deep in his throat, I knew I was wet. My body had deceived me and turned my fear into arousal. The Man lifted his fingers, rubbing the slickness between his thumb and forefingers.

I dropped my head back down onto the bed. My mind and body were at war, unable to decide what I *truly* wanted.

But when he brought his fingers back and slowly eased them inside of me, there was no doubt of what I desired.

The feeling was too euphoric for me to deny. His fingers in me felt like something I'd been waiting for since I stepped foot onto the grounds of *Inferno's Edge*.

With a jolt of my shoulders, The Man glanced up to me, a satisfaction in his eyes.

And dammit, if I didn't love being the cause of it.

He curled his fingers inside of me, pressing against my walls, and my pussy squeezed him in response. His thumb pushed my swollen clit, and I instinctively moaned through the rubber in my mouth.

Slowly, his fingers eased in and out of me as his face remained between my legs. I could tell by the look in his eyes that he wanted to devour me. He wanted to rip his mask off and take me in his mouth, tasting me for all that I am.

But he didn't. He simply used his fingers for my pleasure, finding all the right spots to make me squirm.

My chest heaved as I fought the battle inside of me. He felt incredible, with the way the pads of his fingers rubbed and pushed with the slightest bit of pressure. It was like he was trying to focus on pleasing me, but he was also doing this for control, for ownership, for domination.

I knew what *he* wanted, but what did *I* want?

Fuck, I couldn't think straight.

I could feel my body accepting his movements for my own undoing. It was approaching faster than I expected, so I bucked my hips to meet him and force more pressure from his hand. He quickly read my body language and looked up at me, tilting his head.

He knew I was close.

Peering down at him through my eyelashes, I paused. His gaze held something sinister, something ominous.

I didn't like that look.

Keeping his two fingers inside of me, The Man reached over to the machine closest to him. Only sparing a half a glance at it, he moved his free hand to a dial, turned it, and then hovered over one of the switches. There were a few small gauges on the face of the machine, but only one had a bouncing needle, and it happened to be the one right above his hand. My eyes widened in shock. There was no way this was real.

Right?

A loud, muffled sob erupted from my throat, but The Man paid me no mind.

With my body still teetering on the edge of ecstasy, he curled his fingers inside me, revamping the impending orgasm. Right as I closed my eyes, with a flick of his wrist, The Man turned on the part of the machine connected to me.

Currents ran all through my body, starting from my head and traveling down to my toes. My hands reactively balled into fists as my knees locked. My muscles felt like they were rubber bands ready to snap, and my bones felt like they were made of glass and unable to bend.

The lights in the room pulsed as the machine sucked up all the electricity and forced it into my being.

My mind went blank, my vision turned white, and my hearing was silenced.

And my orgasm ripped through me like a chainsaw, splitting my body in two.

With part of my body fighting the electricity and the other half embracing natural pleasure, I felt like I was entering another realm. One where I couldn't be touched, where I had no demons to fight, and where no one could find me. I was transforming into the light of a storm, destroying everything in my path but leaving nothing broken.

The Man flipped the switch off and removed his fingers from my center. My arched back dropped down onto the bed as my lungs tried to save me with each and every inhale. With my eyes still closed, The Man pulled the mouthguard out of my mouth and threw it onto the floor. A string of spit fell on my chin and ran along my jaw as my mouth remained open, a silent cry echoing into nothing.

The Man pulled the electrodes off my temples and let the cords fall, leaving a lingering buzz in my skin.

I suddenly felt ashamed of the bliss I endured, because it was unlike anything I had ever experienced.

And I wouldn't say no to doing it again.

Rolling my head to the side, I looked to The Man, who was standing close to the edge of the bed. Our eyes met, his shimmering blue locking onto my deep brown. For a moment, I felt like I could read him, understand him, accept him. He must've felt it, too, because he reached down and undid the restraints on my wrists.

Once free, I clasped my hands together, rubbing the skin along my arms as I pulled my sleeves down. My jeans were still down past my knees, and I quickly grabbed them and hiked them back up. I shimmied them up and buttoned them, all while The Man watched. A quick flare of heat spread on my cheeks as I quickly grew embarrassed and ashamed.

But I had to push those feelings away. I couldn't let those emotions take over, at least not now.

As good as everything felt, I needed to get out. I needed to fight back.

I needed to run.

With hesitation in my core, I debated on my next move, and I could tell he was expecting me to try something. Anything. Anticipation flooded the space between us as I glanced down at my boots, making sure they were still secured on my feet. They were.

I looked back up to The Man, who looked as if he was starting to grow bored of me.

I swung my legs over the side of the bed, letting them dangle. My muscles felt so weak, so worn, and I wasn't sure if I could make it out of there. I looked to the door, which was in the corner of the room. In order to get out, I had to make it past The Man first.

It was now or never.

I jumped off the bed and immediately collapsed to the floor, my body weak from the electrocution. My knees slammed on the concrete, followed by my palms, and even my arms couldn't hold me up. My chest flushed against the floor, my bones liquifying under my skin. My muscles were too weak to stand back up, so I tried my best to crawl out of the room. The toe of my boots pushed off the floor, inching me little by little to the exit. Using the rest of my remaining strength, I pulled myself forward, finally making it to the door.

But then, I felt big, firm hands wrap around my ankles as my body slid on the floor.

He was pulling me back.

Growling, I struggled to crawl again, but he continued to pull me back. A light chuckle filtered out from his lips, pissing me off.

I'm glad I could be entertaining.

The new fury he planted in me refueled my strength, and somehow, I managed to scramble my way back up and take off running. It was only a second before there were footsteps behind me.

Right as I got to the back door, his arms wrapped around me again. I tried to grab the door handle, to hold onto it with all my might, but The Man yanked me back.

I clawed at the air, reaching for the door, but I was only an inch or two short.

The Man didn't move. He kept me in his arms as his feet remained in the same spot on the floor.

He wasn't taking me back to the bed, and he wasn't pushing me outside.

He was waiting for me to stop flailing, to stop resisting.

So, with my lungs panting and my eyes watering, I stopped. With a newfound fire in my spine, I straightened up, forcing myself to stand completely still as his arms remained around me.

I closed my eyes as my chest weighed me down, feeling like I could pass out at any second.

The Man leaned his face down into the crook of my shoulder, breathing in the scent of the fear I was emitting. He breathed me in, drank in my dread, and brushed his nose up the length of my neck. And with every one of his exhales, he breathed life back into me.

Goosebumps spread upon every inch of my body, coating me in a layer of fear that only he could give me. I inhaled the moment, feeling like we were on the edge of our elements, waiting to see what was going to happen next.

The Man raised his hand and moved my hair over my shoulder, letting it fall down my back. His masked lips hovered over my ear, almost touching it. It was the most delicate he'd been all night, and I fed into it. I tilted my head ever so slightly, angling myself toward him just a fraction of an inch.

And that's when he said one word to me, his voice so deep and so smooth, so rich and so dark. One word that changed that moment instantly.

"Run."

4:59 AM

Fight or flight was officially activated. Back in *The Asylum*, I chose to fight. Now, with one sharp word ringing in my ear, I chose flight. I flung open the door in front of me and bolted out without looking back. With stumbling steps, I fled, and from what I could hear, The Man didn't follow me. He wasn't running after me, and I don't think he even stepped outside for that matter.

But then again, he didn't have to because I knew he was *always* watching me.

I ran as fast as my legs could carry me, even though my muscles were aching for rest. My knees still felt wobbly, and my blood felt thin. It was like I just woke up from a coma and broke out into a sprint with no time to stretch or warm up.

I came up to *The Vision* and made the split-second decision to keep going. There wasn't much in there besides neon hallways and tilted rooms. If anything, it would hinder my ability to get away from him since everything was so skewed.

I needed balance. I needed consistency.

My lungs felt like they were burning as I continued to pump my legs and run. Leaves crunched under me as I passed the picnic tables and the food trucks. I was running in fear, running away from the person who captured me, running because I was commanded to. It was an odd feeling, knowing there wasn't a single soul around to witness what was happening, even though the place was packed only a few hours ago.

In the dead of night, I had no one to help me.

I came to *The Eternity* and slid into the entrance. I was greeted by the same living room as before- red walls, a couch, lounge chairs, a coffee table with roses, and a bookshelf. Everything was in its proper place, and nothing was smashed or broken. There was absolutely no evidence of what Connor and I had done here earlier. I crouched down to the floor and began pulling out books from the bookshelf, hoping to find what I wanted.

But there was nothing.

There was no baseball bat.

I quickly shoved the books back on the shelf. I tried to make them look somewhat orderly to hide my presence, but I didn't have time. Getting back up to my feet, I ran through the kitchen, past the bedroom, and into the dining room. Every room was back to normal.

Then again, how many laps did we take before we started smashing things?

I *could* press on and keep running, but I didn't want to take the chance of The Man finding me before I could hide.

Glancing up, I looked at the antler chandelier before falling to my knees and crawling under the dining room table. I tucked my trembling legs up to my chest, hugging them tight. With a deep breath, I concentrated on my breathing and tried to keep it steady and quiet.

Inhale, exhale.

Inhale.

Exhale.

My blood was pulsating throughout my entire body. I could feel my heartbeat in all my muscles, including the burning ones in my thighs. I squeezed my eyes shut as I sat in the quiet darkness.

Inhale.

Exhale.

It was only a matter of minutes before I heard a heavy footstep.

My body went rigid, and my heart lodged itself in my throat as I held my breath.

Step, step.

There was nowhere to go. Sitting here, I backed myself into a figurative corner, hoping to remain hidden.

I peeked my eyes open to see his boots make their way into the room. His steps were slow, and his gait was dragging.

Step, Step.

I bit my bottom lip, drawing a drop of blood.

I knew better than to move a single muscle. If there was anything I could do to save me right now, it was to hold completely still. I drew a silent inhale, then eased out a silent exhale.

Step.

His steps stopped at the table. My eyes slowly moved up his legs, but I could only see to his knees.

I licked the blood off my lip, my pulse rushing through me like a tsunami.

The silence hung in the balance between us. He was being as still as me.

And in that moment, I knew.

I just knew.

He found me.

With a quick thrust, two chairs crashed on the floor and skidded across the room. Since he gave me an opening, I decided to use that to my advantage, even though that meant I would be escaping *toward* him. I slid out from under the table and rushed to my feet, not taking a second to look at him, find my balance, or even *breathe*.

I just ran.

I headed for the door, shoved it open, and ran outside.

The cold, thin air hit me like a sheet of glass, cutting my lungs the moment I inhaled. My boots pounded the ground under me as I ran, and this time, I could feel The Man following me. I looked over my shoulder, and sure enough, there he was. His black silhouette blended in with the darkness, and even the whites of his eyes were dimmed under the sudden absence of moonlight. His strides were long, and I knew it wouldn't take long for him to catch up to me.

But still, I ran. My body flipped an invisible switch as it carried me through the park, my endurance lasting longer than I could've expected.

A sweat broke out along my forehead as I made my way to the back of the park. Even though it was already hard to see, looking into the tree line as I approached was absolutely impossible. It was as if a black fog snaked its way through the trees, not giving an ounce of light. I felt like if I were to step foot in there, I would fall into a pit of blackness.

But I had no choice.

He was behind me, and I had nowhere to turn.

I rushed into the woods, throwing myself into the abyss head first. I kept my arms out in front of me, shielding me from any sudden trees or branches. Since using my sight was out of the question, I tried to use a different sense. I felt the hard ground under me and knew I was on the main path. If I stepped a bit to the side, the ground turned soft, letting me know I was veering off. I listened to the crunch of the leaves, the snaps of the branches under me, and the steps of The Man behind me. He was only a few paces behind me, but I was consistently keeping the distance.

If I could get to the other side of these woods, I'd make it to the parking lot, and I would be free.

I could run to the road, I could run to find help, I could run *away from here.*

But as I pushed my way through the trees and branches, I found myself enjoying this.

I enjoyed his dominance.

I enjoyed the rush, the adrenaline, the fear.

I enjoyed the *chase.*

I found myself slowing down a half step, hoping he might bridge the gap between us. But then I kicked my legs even harder, even faster, because I wanted him to fucking *work for it*.

If he was going to take me, I wasn't going to make it easy.

With my eyes adjusted to the darkness, my surroundings started to look less like vague trees and leaves and more like a place I'd been before. Things looked familiar. I slowed my run down to a jog as I processed the space around me, not noticing that the footsteps behind me were silent.

I knew I'd been in these woods before; that part was obvious. But the fact that I was trailing the same path as before, out of hundreds of acres, couldn't be a coincidence. Either my subconscious led me this way, or I was being led without even realizing it.

Taking a slow, easy step forward, I glanced to the ground before me, where a tree root arched up from the dirt. My eyes only acknowledged its existence for half a second before turning my head away.

It was then that I was hyperaware of the silence. There was no one pursuing me, at least not with physical steps. I wasn't brought here accidentally. I was corralled into this area in hopes that I would make the same mistakes twice.

I wouldn't.

Doing my best to try and act nervous, I franticly glanced around the forest. I pretended to look for a way out, a way away, or a way to hide. In my search around the trees, my eyes fell upon the toe of a rounded black boot, nearly blending into the night if it wasn't for the silver lace holes along the front.

He was crouched in the shadows, waiting for me to trip.

I approached the tree root, acting as if I had no memory of it. Swallowing my anticipation, I took one final step before throwing my foot into his space, hoping to make contact with his body and send him flying.

But instead of him toppling over as I had hoped, he grabbed my ankle and pulled me forward, causing me to lose my balance and fall to the ground. Thankfully, my hands caught my weight, and I saved myself from landing completely on my back.

I let out a frustrated growl. He was always one fucking step ahead, knowing my next move before I even did.

His hands remained around my boot as I tried to kick again and again. I looked like a toddler having a tantrum, but I didn't care. I would do anything to get out of his grasp.

One of my kicks had enough push to send him backward, momentarily releasing my leg. There was a sharp rip sound through the air, and I watched as he turned to look. The back of his black sleeve was ripped vertically, exposing a bloodied arm. Behind him was the broken and splintered tree trunk, the same one I almost hurt myself on earlier. The Man turned his arm, showing a gash that matched the rip with blood running down his exposed flesh.

I couldn't help but smile. I wounded him.

I somehow managed to crack his armor.

His eyes flared with an animosity that I hadn't seen tonight, and I took that as my cue to run. Standing up and turning on my heel, I ran on the path, jumping over the fishing wire that would activate the net. I heard The Man behind me jump over the line as well.

If he wanted to catch me, he was going to do it with his own hands. Not a net.

I took a hard right, leading him off the worn trail and into heavy foliage. He followed me, listening to my movements as we both struggled to find our way through nature's maze. Branches scratched my face, and I could feel minor cuts forming on my cheeks and forehead.

After what seemed like miles, a glimmer of something caught my eye. It was far ahead, but it was noticeable, and I'll go for anything noticeable at this point. Especially something in this darkness.

I followed what I saw and soon noticed it was bright red.

It wasn't moving, it wasn't small but it wasn't large, and it had an odd circular shape.

Once I got close enough, I knew exactly what it was.

It was paint splatter.

Paint from the paintball guns when Connor and I were here.

I reached out and touched the dry paint as I passed the tree, then I resumed my sprint.

It was all the motivation I needed to find my way out.

5:17 AM

Right before dawn is always the darkest. And now that I've found my footing, I didn't need to fear the dark. Since I was here once before, I knew exactly where I was heading and how to get there. I just needed to stay ahead.

My boots kicked up the dirt beneath me, leaving a trail of imprints for The Man to follow.

I tried to look for the cave that Connor and I found. Maybe it could offer some hidden shelter, a hiding spot away from The Man's pursuit. But as I continued on, nothing seemed to look familiar anymore. Did I wander off the path I was on before? Did I miss the signs, the guides, the paint on the trees? I searched around me, looking for the black abyss covered in moss, but I couldn't see any hint of it anywhere.

I bit my bottom lip. I needed to find it if I didn't want to be caught.

Then again, The Man probably knew where it was and how to get there with his eyes closed. I'm sure it would be the first place he would look for me.

I struggled to catch my breath as I continued on, but I couldn't hear The Man breathing heavily at all. It's as if he wasn't fazed by this in the slightest.

This was child's play to him.

As I headed in the direction of the parking lot, I noticed things got quiet. There were no footsteps behind me, no strong presence at my back.

But I kept going, not letting it trip me up as I felt my way through the woods.

I could feel a change in the ground below me, and I knew I was returning to the worn path. Part of me didn't want to place myself where I could be easily found, but the other part of me was exhausted. I was done pushing myself through sharp branches, bushes with thorns, and uneven ground.

So, I stepped onto the path and held my breath, even though my lungs were screaming for me to breathe.

I tried to remain light and keep my steps quiet. But there was something off about where I was.

I glanced over my shoulder, trying to see if there was something I missed.

But as I kept walking, something bumped into my face.

I turned back around to see a foot.

A foot.

I looked up and screamed, my voice rattling through the trees and settling on the leaves.

It was the man who had hung himself earlier.

He was still here. His face was pale, his mouth was open, and his body swung in the light breeze.

In all the other houses, everything was cleaned up and back to normal. There was no smeared blood, broken glass, or hidden baseball bats. The stage was set for the next set of people who wanted to claim their experience.

But here, deep in the secluded, abandoned forest, someone hung from a rope, waiting to be found. He was alone in his death, his soul broken in a life that had no other solution.

My legs finally gave out, both from exhaustion and fear. I expected to fall on the dirt, but I didn't. My arms caught on something that held me up.

One whiff of sandalwood, and I knew exactly who had me.

The Man kept me off the ground, his arms hooked under my shoulders, as he dragged me backward. I tried to turn my body and kick, but it was useless. I was tired and sore. My bones ached from exhaustion and lack of rest.

My feet found their way back to the ground, and using The Man as leverage, I stood up. With one swift motion, he turned his body, bent at the waist, and pushed his shoulder into my stomach. He hoisted me up, carrying me like a heaping bag of sand. I wanted to kick and thrash and squirm my way out of his hold, but I knew his strength would overpower mine. I've been fighting this whole night, both physically and mentally, and I knew that my own stamina was diminishing.

With his arm tightly secured around my thighs, he carried me to an opening, where there was a flat boulder about a foot off the ground encased by trees. Once we were at the smooth rock, he dropped me and forced me down onto my stomach, the side of my face squished along the rock's surface. Not once did I expect him to be gentle with me, but feeling him toss me like a ragdoll wounded any hopes I had.

"What do you want from me, *huh?*" I yelled over my shoulder, my throat scratchy and sore from the screams, my face barely lifted off the rock.

It was a dumb question because I knew what he wanted. With the bulge in his jeans and the lust in his eyes, he made it clear that he wanted me.

All of me.

Even with my clothes that were ripped, scuffed, and covered in blood, dirt, and paint. Even with the scratches that freckled my face and the leaves that intertwined themselves in my hair.

He stared at me as he crouched to my level on the side of the rock. His hand found its way under my chin, and he turned my face to look at him.

There was a sliver of dawn breaking through behind him, and I knew our time was almost up.

Daylight was coming.

With a quick twist of my hips, I turned and planted my boot on his chest, shoving him backward. He lost his balance for only a moment before righting himself.

Then, moving onto his knees, he slowly made his way to me, and my smile dropped.

Oh, *fuck*.

His eyes shined in the hint of daybreak, glistening with anticipation and expectation.

I went to kick him again, but this time, he caught my ankle and stopped my force. He pulled me to the edge of the rock, wedging himself between my legs in the process.

And that's when I knew he had me.

Here, in the middle of the autumn-colored woods, with the morning glow on the horizon, I was his.

My pussy tightened at the thought.

Not wasting any time, The Man reached up and tore open my jeans, ripping off the button and sending it flying. He yanked them down to my knees, then stepped over them and pushed them down to my ankles. I released a whimper as the cold air hit my skin, goosebumps rising on every inch of my legs.

My eyes looked up to the trees above, where I noticed something hanging and swaying gently from a branch. I squinted while trying to focus on the object before finally realizing what it was.

A set of antlers hung from a rope, clinking against the tree next to me.

With an exhale, I welcomed the sight. It was almost like a comfort to me now, a consistency in this world of madness.

I was brought back down to the moment as The Man buried his masked face between my legs, letting his nose brush against the inside of my thighs before moving up to my underwear. I could hear him draw in a deep breath, inhaling my fear, anticipation, and lust.

I placed my hands on his shoulders, his *huge fucking shoulders*, and tried to push him off. My palms shoved him away, but his core strength was too strong for me.

Then, he slipped a gloved finger under the waistband of my underwear, sending a jolt through the sensitive skin in my hip, and hooked the fabric in his grip. With an upward pull, he ripped it clean off.

And I stopped trying to push him away because the move made me so *fucking* wet.

A small moan escaped me as the brisk air hit my exposed skin. The Man took me in, drank in the sight of me, then slowly moved up my body. His arms, his covered face, and his gloved hands all roamed over me, savoring me, taking pleasure in this everlasting moment. My muscles tensed under his smooth, gentle touch before he turned rough and rugged. He grabbed my arms and moved them above my head, locking my wrists together between one of his hands and the boulder. My eyes met his, only for a moment, before his face dove into the crook of my neck. My eyes fluttered closed as his breath caressed my delicate skin, sending a new, unlocked rapture through my entire body.

Somewhere in my head, I registered the sound of him undoing his belt, but the euphoria in the rush made me forget about everything. I had no reluctance and no resistance for him. I rode the wave of my fears and focused on the satisfaction that awaited me.

With my eyes closed, The Man's face still buried in my neck, and his body nestled between my legs, he shoved his throbbing cock deep inside me.

I let out a gasp as I felt him perfectly aligned with me, filling me in all the exact places I wanted him to be.

He was *made for me.*

He thrust again, his hips smooth and his movements effortless.

I could feel his bare skin against mine. There was no barrier between us, no protection, and it felt incredible. Indescribable. I lifted my hips to meet him, and I could feel his body slowly sink into mine. We were both vulnerable in this moment, with our bodies exposed and our souls entwined, connecting in the most organic way possible. I tried to lower my arms, but his grip was unrelenting as he continued to hold them high, not letting me have any type of control over the situation.

I tilted my chin up, allowing him more room to explore my neck. My eyes remained closed as he brushed his nose against the front of my throat, toying with his prey in the heat of the moment.

And I allowed it.

I *wanted* it.

His cock pulsed deep inside as he penetrated me, his length longer than I could accommodate. My walls wrapped around him, squeezing him, and I could feel his entire body shudder.

I wanted all of him; I wanted his cock, his cum, and his lust, but I also wanted his eyes, his mouth, and his bare hands on me. I wanted to see him, see who he really was, see the look on his face when his eyes met mine.

But instead, he continued to fuck me, and I continued to softly groan in his ear, the sounds like a soundtrack to his primal fervor. My ass scraped against the rock as The Man's knees dug into the ground; his height perfectly matched with my position.

I began to cry out as my body began to succumb to its needs. I could feel myself growing more and more sensitive with each thrust, my clit swelling every time his skin would brush against it.

The Man's free hand roamed all over my body, from under my knee to my hip, from my breast up to my jaw. He would go from a gentle touch to a harsh grasp in less than a second. The unpredictability of it all had me in an emotional whiplash.

With an arch of my back and a slight lift of my legs, The Man hit the spot that sent me into a spiral. The orgasm ripped through my entire body as every muscle tightened at the sensation. My heart nearly combusted at the bliss, beating every ounce of blood throughout my body with excessive speed. An instinctive cry mixed itself with a low, wrecked moan as it filtered its way out of me. The Man closed his eyes as he dropped his head, his thrusts matching mine as he followed me over the edge, filling me. His body tried to collapse onto mine, but somehow, he kept his composure and held himself over me. I studied his breathing, his chest heavy and quick, and realized this was the only time during the night when he lost himself. He gave every part of himself to me, including his drive and desperation.

I watched him through heavy eyelids as he brought his face back over mine, his eyes soft but piercing through the depths of his drive. He let go of my wrists, but my body was too relaxed and exhausted to move them. They went limp above my head, still crossed in their X formation.

His hand moved down to my face as his fingers brushed my hair away from my cheek.

And that's when my eyes fluttered closed, my body giving in to darkness as daylight streamed into the forest.

PART THREE

Northern lights carried me to you and will carry us through.
With your hair under the touch of my hand, I will take you.
And I will break you.

10:34 AM

Ice clinked against glass, the delicate sound waking me. My eyes opened slowly, blinking a few times before focusing on nothing but white. I blinked again, looking to both sides.

Where am I?

It took me a minute to gain my bearings. I was lying on my back, but I was comfortable. There was softness all around me, and my head and neck were propped up slightly.

I was in a bed.

I looked around again.

It was *my* bed, and I woke up to *my* ceiling.

Slowly sitting up, I winced at the pain shooting through my body. My shoulders were aching, my back was tight, and my side was burning.

My side?

Confused, I pulled the covers off and looked down, lifting the oversized shirt to see my skin. There was a giant welt about the size of a softball above my right hip.

And that's when the delirium wore off, leaving me to remember everything that happened overnight.

Now that I remembered, there was no way I could ever forget.

I pushed the blankets away as I stretched, doing my best to avoid pulling any more muscles than I already had. But as I pushed my arms out in front of me, I noticed red, raw skin circling my wrists. My eyes moved up the length of my forearms, where more scratches and bruises began.

I looked down to my bare legs, where more cuts were dashed in my flesh, some of them even filled with speckles of dirt.

As I was studying myself, a pleasant, subtle smell hit me, filling the space around me. I glanced over to see a tray placed on the end table next to my bed. There was a glass of water with drips of condensation trailing down the outside as the ice continued to shift and tap the insides. A plate of bacon, a few pancakes, and a bowl of fruit also sat on the tray, looking more appetizing than ever.

My stomach growled. I was *starving*.

Reaching for a grape, I popped it in my mouth as I noticed a note. It was a folded paper next to a bouquet of white roses in a beautiful black vase. As my heart did a miniature flip, I smiled at the sight and picked up the note, chewing on my fruit.

For You.

X

I placed the paper down, keeping my grin, and popped another grape in my mouth. The fruit was still cold, and the pancakes were still warm. The food must have arrived only a few minutes ago, at most.

A sound echoed from across the room, causing me to snap my head at the noise. It came from the door that led to the master bathroom. My heart thudded at the noise.

Picking up one last piece of fruit, I climbed out of bed and softly padded toward the door. My bare legs were suddenly cold as I made my way across the room, silently and slowly, the shirt I was wearing falling down to the middle of my thighs. Once I reached the door, I placed one palm on it gently while the other rested on the handle.

Sounds of dripping, draining water filtered through the wooden door.

It was the shower.

Turning the knob, I opened the door, a flood of steam hitting me immediately. I squinted through the heated fog and stepped into the bathroom, the tile cold under my feet.

There, through the glass shower doors and under the spray of the water, was a man.

A tall man with broad shoulders, strong arms, and long legs.

As he faced away from me, his head hung under the water, the streams running down his face and neck and flowing from his short, dark hair. My eyes trailed along his entire being, leading me down the length of his tattooed body before he turned to the side.

Water cascaded down the bridge of his nose as he closed his eyes, his face angled to the floor.

And that's when I saw his right arm and a giant cut down the back of it.

10:40 AM

Excitement soared through every inch of me at the sight of him. Lifting my shirt, I peeled it off, leaving me naked and bare. As I quietly stepped toward the shower, I studied him and the ink that spread across his body. He had a beautiful, intricate picture of a forest that covered the whole slate of his back, but my eyes locked on the design that stretched along the top of his shoulders. Thick, solid black lines ran in both directions, some slightly curved as they reached from one side to the other, some even pointed up toward the back of his neck.

Antlers.

I grinned at the design.

I slid open the door and moved to step in when he turned to look at me. His eyes devoured me, his sight pinned to me with no plans of moving away. I could see his vision focus on the tiny cuts along my face from this morning's adventure. Whatever he was thinking about my roughed appearance wasn't deterring him in the slightest, the rise of his cock clear and unmistakable proof.

I closed the glass door behind me, never taking my gaze off him. Then, with one swift movement, he wrapped his hand around the back of my skull and guided me to the wall, cradling me, making sure I didn't hit my head on the tile. I stood under the spray of the water, my side and my back getting the most of it as I let the warmness drape over me like a blanket.

Without speaking, he fell before me to his knees, and that action in itself said more to me than words ever could.

I looked down at him, with his crystal blue eyes and his short, dark hair, and forced myself to stay upright. Between his sharp cheekbones, his wide, rounded shoulders, and his sculpted chest, there was no chance for me to keep calm. His lips caressed my clit, his movements so subtle but effective. I tried to grip the wall, but there was nothing to hold onto, so I simply held onto his shoulders. He grunted at my touch, the quick jolt of his cock a sign that I clearly had the same impact on him that he had on me.

I rolled my head back at the feeling of his mouth on me. I savored it as my jaw dropped, the feeling of breathlessness taking over me. He slid his tongue up, licking me gently and leaving no place untouched. He pushed two fingers inside me easily, the pressure taking me to new highs that only climbed higher.

I fought the urge to throw my leg over his shoulder. Instead, I balanced on my tip toes, keeping my weight on the balls of my feet.

It was like he was able to read me because right as I let out a cry, he stood to his feet and wrapped an arm around me, catching me as my knees gave way. I leaned back, letting him hold my weight as we stared at each other. His eyes scanned all of me, from my face to the water dripping down my neck, from my breasts to the discolored bruise on my side. His eyebrows slanted down at the sight, and with gentle fingertips, he traced the circle on my skin. A disappointing glance flashed on his face, but the look was fleeting.

Then, without hesitation, he kissed me.

His lips were strong and fierce, soft and full. I matched his intensity, letting the return of my kiss fit right into his. Our tongues danced, our noses brushed, all while our naked, slick bodies pressed into each other. I could feel his cock nestled against my stomach, pulsing with need and aching to be relieved. I reached down and grabbed it, his body tensing at the touch, and began to stroke him. He was thick, long, and harder than I'd ever felt him before.

His hands came up and cupped my breasts, the shower water coating them and falling into his palms. He took both nipples in between his fingers, pinching lightly. I let out a breathless whimper, my needs exposed to him. He leaned down and took one of the nipples between his lips, running his tongue along the bud and almost making me come right on the spot.

Standing back upright, he pinned me to the wall, lifting me slightly. He pulled one of my legs up, his palm under the bend of my knee, spreading my legs wide open for him.

His eyes moved down to my center, and his lips curled up into a small smile.

Then, with one quick, effortless thrust, he shoved himself inside me. His hips met mine, and we both let out a moan; our feelings matched, and our souls connected. He pumped himself in me with the utmost need and desire, my blood heating through me with each crash of our bodies.

I curled my hands around his arms, using him to keep myself up but also reveling in the feeling of his skin under mine. I ran my hands down the back of his arm, skimming along the giant gash and the start of the scab that was beginning to form. The feeling of it only sent me higher, the euphoria climbing higher in the mountains of my chest, tearing me open from the inside out.

His fingertips trailed down my body, landing on the top of my clit as his thumb circled it slowly. I closed my eyes, letting him do his work to me as he continued to thrust, his desperation for me evident.

I felt myself tip to the edge, as if I was outside my body looking down at the valley below.

And then I fell.

My body wracked through a deep orgasm, shaking against the person who gave it to me. I felt myself go weak in his arms, and my knees gave out as I let the wave take me, wash me, cleanse me, and swallow me.

Reading my body, he followed suit, his thrusts turning shallow and losing their rhythm. I felt the warmness of his cum inside me, coating me as the water from the shower covered us.

He looked to me, and I to him, unspoken words flowing in the space between us. Then he smiled, the effortless grin filling my heart with everything I could ever ask for.

11:12 AM

Nighttime memories came rushing back to me as I sat on the edge of my bed, chewing on a small piece of cantaloupe.

The haunted houses.

The falling, the running, the smashing.

The 3D glasses.

The elevator.

The bloody woman in the bathtub.

The fog, the bracelets, the trivia questions.

The rubber tunnel.

Mia finding me in the bathroom.

Elliot disappearing in *The Eternity*.

Connor protecting me in *The Night*.

It was an experience I'll *never* forget.

The bathroom door opened, and a flood of steam clouded the bedroom as he stepped out in just a towel. I looked up from my breakfast and smirked. Drips of water dropped off his dark, wet hair and ran down onto his glistening, inked chest.

I lifted a hand, motioning to the array of food. "You didn't have to do this for me."

He didn't even think twice before responding, his voice deep and velvety. "Of course I did. It's what we always do."

His long legs led him across the room to the dresser, where he proceeded to drop his towel and get dressed. The sight of his naked body sent familiar heatwaves to the pit of my stomach, and I reveled in the glow.

I looked back to the half-eaten pancakes, an empty plate of bacon, and a dwindling bowl of fruit. I reached for a strawberry and bit into it with a soft, juicy crunch. He always spoiled me after a night out, as a thank you, as a reassurance that the night was only play.

It was always just play.

Every November 1ˢᵗ begins a new year at *Inferno's Edge*. The park is closed for renovations, upgrades, and remodeling. Floor plans change, themes are switched up, and new ideas are tossed around. The park is a year-round business with an excellent team of innovators who strive to switch things up and remain the top set of haunted houses in America.

And it's all led by *him*.

He oversees every change, every issue, every addition and alteration. He hires those he trusts, who can help him with things like paychecks, insurance, and marketing. He approves every detail that goes into each house, down to the color of the walls and the placements of the lasers.

And once October 1ˢᵗ comes around and the park is open to the public, he is done.

He is no longer the businessman who runs the park.

He is *The Man.*

He is my predator, and I am his prey.

He is my captor, and I am his victim.

He is my love, and I am his.

With one leg dangling over the side of the bed and the other tucked under me, I turned my shoulders to face him.

"You've outdone yourself this year," I said with a smile, reaching for the fruit and popping another grape in my mouth. Last night was night one of the Halloween season, and this year's houses at *Inferno's Edge* did *not* disappoint.

"I'm glad you enjoyed it," his gravelly voice carried across the room to me, the sound quickly finding its way right into my core.

I mumbled under my breath. "I think we both know I did a little more than enjoy it."

Even though his back was to me, I could see his smile run throughout his entire body. The way his muscles tightened, then released with ease, told me all I needed to know. He enjoyed it just as much as I did.

"How did we even get back here last night?" I asked, propping myself up on one hand, the other hand brushing along the blankets on the bed. "I don't remember anything after the woods."

He grabbed a pair of dark jeans and pulled them on, hesitating before answering. "I carried you. You were exhausted."

"You *carried* me?" I asked, shocked.

He turned to look at me over his shoulder, confused at my surprise. "We weren't far away. I only carried you up the back hill to the house."

Our house, the only house that rests right along the outskirts of the forest and hides in the back of the lot. We live here so we can have easy access to the haunted houses and can show up whenever needed, which is more often than not.

And even though we live on the property, I still can never find my way around those damn woods. I've been through them a few times, but I don't come close to having them memorized like he does, and I don't have a desire to. It's part of the reason why our special nights turn out so perfect- it's because I legitimately can never find my way out of the woods.

A memory from last night—*this morning*—popped into my head, and I sat up straighter at the thought.

"I found a cave." I grinned and raised my eyebrows, impressed with myself.

The rumors were true; they existed on the property. But the stories of people getting lost in them and never finding their way out certainly *weren't* true. In fact, they may or may not have been made up by those of us who work here just to add to the mysterious lore.

And even though they were real, and even though I lived on the land that had them, I had never found one.

Until last night.

"Oh, yeah?" he asked, amused. "Did you go in?"

"Hell no. I'd probably never find my way out."

A dark, slight chuckle played on his lips. "Don't worry," he assured, his gaze eclipsing in obscurity, making my pulse begin to race. "I'd find you, *fuck you*, then drag you out of there screaming."

My breath hitched in my throat as I pictured it. Him, dressed as dark as the inside of the cave, taking all of me while I'm unable to see *anything*.

Waiting for his next move.

Itching to find my way out.

Fighting him off.

Feeling. Submitting.

Letting go.

Maybe that will be my goal next time. Find the cave, go in, hide, and wait. A small giggle tried to crawl its way out of me at the thought, but I suppressed it down.

Sometimes, I liked to plan little things in our fun nights, too.

As he grabbed a grey short-sleeved shirt, I snapped out of my fantasies and glanced at the vertical gash in his arm, my eyes leading down the slashed skin that caused a deep line in the black ink.

"Does it hurt?" I asked.

He shook his head. "No. You got me good, though."

I winced. "Sorry."

A slight grin spread on his lips as he turned to me, pulling his shirt down over his toned stomach. "Don't be. Last night was incredible." He stepped over and sat on the bed beside me, taking my chin in his hand. "*You* were incredible."

I exhaled, even though the guilt was still breathing through me. "I'll buy you a new sweatshirt."

A laugh escaped him, the sound like music to my ears. "No, you won't. You'll rest your pretty little ass right here, all day."

"I can buy the sweatshirt on my phone, you know. I don't even have to get out of bed to do it."

"Baby," he began, the smile still on his face, showing his perfect, white teeth. "You're not buying me anything. Don't even think about it."

Before I could fight back, he leaned in and kissed me, his lips so incredibly soft and full. Slowly, he wrapped his arm around me and tried to lay me back down on the bed, but my body tightened when his hand grazed over my welt. He noticed my quick flinch and stopped.

A heavy silence floated over us both as he pulled away from me and leaned back, his finger moving up to his bottom lip in thought. I was sore, yes, but the feeling wasn't as bad as I was expecting. The mark was only surface deep, and the bruise under it looked a lot worse than it felt.

But before I could defend my strength, he spoke up.

"I fired Joss."

His words cut the stillness between us, and my mouth dropped wide open. "What? Why?"

He looked down at my side before slightly lifting the shirt I was wearing, showing the bruise. "That's why."

I stared at him, floored by this information. Joss was one of our closest friends and helped us grow *Inferno's Edge*. He was there the first year we opened and has been there every year since. He's been an actor, a man behind the scenes, and everything in between.

"He's the one that hit you with the paintball. I told him to aim for the guy you were with, but he missed, even though he was at close fucking range. So, I fired him."

I dropped my shoulders in defeat. "You can't—"

"No," he said, cutting me off. "Joss knew the rules. You're off limits. Anyone that hurts you is gone."

The ice in his eyes was real, and I could feel the coldness in his stare. I sighed. There was no convincing him otherwise, even though firing Joss was a mistake.

"And because I was too busy ripping Joss a new asshole, I didn't have time to cut the SynCad down from the tree."

"SynCad?" I asked, puzzled.

"Synthetic cadaver."

My heart skipped a beat. The man who hung himself in the tree. Even though he was still there when we ran through the forest for the second time, it was only because no one had time to straighten up after Connor and I left. I shuddered at the memory of it all.

"Yeah, that definitely caught me off guard."

"I know, and I'm sorry. After the place closes, it's supposed to be just you and me with no distractions."

He paused before giving me more reassurance.

"You and me. It's only us."

I stared at him as he spoke, the realization dawning on me. He remembered that no one cut the cadaver down, so when I saw it for the second time, he knew I wouldn't be expecting it, and he knew he had to be there to catch me when I fell.

And he did.

Throughout all our play, throughout the entire night, he was always looking out for me, even if he had an odd way of showing it.

He would never let fear *completely* take me.

He was my protector, even if it seemed like I needed protection away from him.

I reached for another piece of fruit and bit into it. "Well, whatever you were trying to achieve, it worked. It looked extremely real."

"Good. It was supposed to. Those things cost a fuck ton of money."

I swallowed the food and then placed the rest of it back on the tray. I gently swiped away some juice from the corner of my mouth as I struggled to find what I wanted to say. The room grew unusually quiet at the sudden change in emotion.

He must've read my expression because his face turned serious.

"What is it?" he asked as his tattooed hand shook off excess water from the back of his head.

My words lingered inside me a few moments longer, causing his look to turn from curious to worried and his movements to still entirely.

"What's wrong, baby? Talk to me."

His blue eyes searched mine, desperate to find an answer.

Lifting my chin up slightly, my voice was soft. "That cadaver wasn't what scared me the most last night."

Silence filled the air, and I continued.

"The gun," I whispered so quietly that he almost couldn't hear it.

Immediately, he took my hands in his. "Why didn't you stop me?" he asked, his eyes wide and pleading, his stare echoing in the depths of my being.

I shrugged and looked down at our fingers intertwining, even though I could feel his continued stare linger on my face. "Because we discussed it already, and because I trust you."

"Oh, absolutely *fucking* not. Baby, please look at me," he said as he softly grasped my chin in his hand, his thumb brushing along my jaw. "I checked and rechecked it before finding you. There were no bullets. None in the clip, none in the chamber. I made sure of it."

He sighed, but it was a concerned movement.

"But more importantly, the *second* you feel any ounce of real fear or hesitation, you call the whole thing off."

"But I—"

"No 'but's. You're in charge. You say the word, and I drop everything."

I nodded silently.

"Say it for me. Say our word, so I know you're with me."

I looked at him directly in the eyes, a fierceness firing through me as I held all the power in one simple word.

"Antlers."

He gave a smooth, reassuring look. "It's why they're everywhere. It's a reminder, for *you,* that you *always* have a way out."

"Speaking of a way out," I began, tilting my head. "Can I ask you something?"

He nodded. "Anything."

"The Eternity." My mind thought back to the house and everything that happened.

The circles, the woman, the chairs on the ceiling.

Elliot and Mia getting lost, Elliot finding his way out, and Mia showing up where she wasn't supposed to.

The baseball bat, the key, the bracelets.

Through it all, there was one nagging question I couldn't shake.

"How did you do it? I can figure out all the other houses without a problem. But I can't wrap my head around the layout of that one. How was it set up? How did we get out when we did?"

He watched me as I spoke, his lips curling up in amusement at all the thoughts spilling out of me like liquid.

But instead of answering me, he simply shrugged, stood to his feet, and sent me a wink.

"Some things are better left as a mystery."

Towering over me, he slowly crawled over me, gently forcing me back on the bed. I lay under him as he moved onto the mattress, letting his body canopy me in protection.

"I have to head back over there for a few hours. One of the lights in *The Vision* is fucked." He gave me a soft nod. "Get some rest."

My hair fanned out on the bed under me as I tilted my head, already ignoring his command. I couldn't help it; he was too captivating with his icy stare, his tightened jaw, and his perfect smile. He could hold me in his hand, and I would melt in it every time.

Every side of him met my needs, whether it was pampering me in the morning, lying in bed with me during the day, or acting out my fears at night.

My hands floated to the skin above the hem of his jeans, my fingertips brushing lightly, and his muscles tensed at my touch. His lust-filled eyes locked with mine, sensing my tease, tasting it on his tongue.

My voice dropped down low, my words gliding from my lips effortlessly, testing him in this moment. "I'll rest in November."

With his hands propping himself up on either side of me, he shook his head and smiled, as if he couldn't believe I had the energy to keep this up. His thumb brushed along a lock of my hair as he quietly spoke. "Does that mean I'll see you again tonight?"

Without hesitation, I nodded. The chase was like a drug to me, and for one month out of the year, I couldn't get enough. Any chance I had, I was taking it.

A sudden fire lit in his eyes as another thought occurred to him. His temperament instantly changed to stone as he turned serious.

"If some other guy tries to lay his hands on you, I won't be so lenient this time around."

I peered up at him, a subtle, playful smirk easing its way onto my lips. "Are you jealous?"

He stared at me with a rigid expression, the muscle in his jaw flexing with intensity. "I fucking mean it. He won't live to see the end of *The Night.*"

I exhaled. "Connor was sweet. He was just looking out for me, that's all."

"Being sweet doesn't get you anywhere. And he wasn't looking out for you; he was looking out for *Sadie.*"

The name. *Sadie.* Last night, it seemed to stick to me perfectly. Maybe I was a Sadie in a past life. Maybe I'll be a Sadie again another night.

Reaching over to the bowl of fruit, I grabbed the last two grapes. I popped one in my mouth, then reached up and pushed the other one past his lips. He took it, bit it, chewed and swallowed it. I did the same and grinned.

"Sadie," I echoed. "I've always liked that name."

With a tip of his chin, he questioned me. "What will your next name be?" he asked, his finger moving to my bottom lip. He pulled it down softly, studying my mouth. I could feel the quick pulse of his cock against my bare thigh.

"I'm not sure. I like the 'S' names, though. Sabrina, maybe?"

"Well, whoever you'll be," he began, moving his head down to hover over my ear. His low voice dropped to a whisper, and my eyes fluttered closed. "I'll find you. I'll catch you. I'll fuck you."

10:43 PM

Darkness swallowed the sky as I walked along the pathway. Leaves were crunching under me with each step as the sweet, seasonal smell of pumpkin spice filled the air around me. I passed a food truck where they made pumpkin-spiced funnel cakes, and I made a mental note to buy one the next time I was here.

I came upon a small, black building and stepped inside. It was dark, with sconces along the walls and black and white mosaic tile on the floor. A few girls washed their hands at the sink, and I politely smiled at them. They looked at me in the mirror as they dried their hands, then proceeded to exit, leaving me alone.

Counting the stalls, I found the fourth door and pushed it open. As I crouched down, my hands slid under the toilet paper dispenser, and my fingers felt a small plastic box.

It was still here.

Perfect.

I pressed a button on the side, turning it on, and a subtle beep echoed through the stalls. Then, I pulled out my phone and connected it to the box via Bluetooth.

Leaving the stall and shutting and locking the door from the outside, I stood patiently with my phone in my hands.

And I waited.

And waited.

And waited as the night grew long.

A few girls came and went, too young for me to join.

Some older women eyed me, but they didn't seem very welcoming.

So, I stood against the frame of the stall, with my head back against the metal, and sighed.

Maybe tonight would be a night where I didn't tag along with anyone.

Those nights happened more often than not, and if they did, I didn't sweat it too much. I would text him and call the whole thing off. We would go home, make some popcorn, watch a scary movie, and fuck until we fell asleep. It was just as good as any other night, and it was exactly what I was expecting until something changed.

A short, blonde girl walked into the bathroom, glancing my way and sending me a friendly smile. I returned the gesture, and once she was in her stall, I quickly straightened up. I pulled up a voice app on my phone and opened it.

"Bec, are you okay?" I asked, my voice tight and worried.

Then, I pressed a button, and a voice poured through the speaker. "Yeah, I'm fine."

"You don't sound fine, Becca."

I scrolled through the premade clips to find what I needed. I clicked on a groan sound, then continued scrolling. Searching for the correct response, I quickly read through them and tapped the one I wanted.

"You should go without me."

The blonde girl came out of her stall and made her way to the sink. With my phone in my hands and my back against the metal, I narrowed my eyebrows.

"What? I can't go without you," I whined, easily selling the act.

At that moment, I looked up at the mirror the blonde girl was standing in front of. We briefly made eye contact, and she sent me a look. It was a look of sympathy, but it was also filled with contemplation.

And I knew that look well.

I was in.

Escaping me will never happen. I will find you, no matter where
you are, and I will keep you inside me.
As the night grows long, you grow closer to me.
In the dead of night, we come alive.
And we run.